GOOD GRIEF...
THIRD GRADE

Also by Colleen O'Shaughnessy McKenna:

Camp Murphy

The Brightest Light

Mother Murphy

The Truth About Sixth Grade

Merry Christmas, Miss McConnell!

Murphy's Island

Fifth Grade: Here Comes Trouble

Eenie, Meanie, Murphy, No!

Fourth Grade Is a Jinx

Too Many Murphys

GOOD GRIEF... THIRD GRADE

COLLEEN O'SHAUGHNESSY McKENNA

Interior illustrations by Richard Williams

A
LITTLE APPLE
PAPERBACK

SCHOLASTIC INC.
New York Toronto London Auckland Sydney

ISBN 0-590-45124-3

22 21 20 19 18 17 16   9/9 0 1/0

Printed in the U.S.A.   40

This book is dedicated to my beautiful sister
Sherrie, who inspires us all by seeing
the best in every "good grief" situation.

Chapter
<u>One</u>

Marsha leaned back in her chair and looked around her third-grade classroom. Today was the first day of school and Mrs. Byrnes was finishing a new bulletin board. It was filled with apples. Each apple was slightly different and had the name of a student in Room 10. Mrs. Byrnes was a very good artist. Marsha was glad she had Mrs. Byrnes for third grade, and not Mrs. Lodge in Room 9. Mrs. Lodge *never* let the kids in her homeroom get drinks. Not even when they had tacos for lunch. Marsha opened her desk. Not one crayon was broken, not one pencil was bitten. Everything was fresh.

Third grade was going to be a fresh start, too. Marsha had promised her parents over breakfast that she wasn't going to get in any trouble in the third grade. She had even decorated a sheet of white paper with roses and rainbows and printed: *I, Marsha Cessano, promise to be very, very good all year long.* She'd signed it and given it to her parents. Boy, were they happy. Mrs. Cessano stuck it on the refrigerator with her favorite magnet. Third grade was going to be the beginning of straight A's, neat desks, and never, ever again being sent down to the principal's office. This year, Sister Mary Elizabeth would have to find somebody else to wave her finger at. By Christmastime, Sister Mary Elizabeth might pick Marsha to carry the poinsettia plant for the manger scene. Marsha knew her parents would be happy. Her gramma might even come to watch. Her parents would tell everyone that Marsha was doing a great job in the third grade. Since she was an only child, they had to count on her for *all* their proud moments. It was kind of a hard job, being an only child.

"Well, look what we have here!"

Marsha didn't even look up. She knew it was rude old Roger Friday, trying to get her mad. He was good at it, too. Too bad his parents hadn't moved to New Mexico over the weekend, or a large dog hadn't picked up Roger by his scrawny neck and run off to Michigan. No such luck. Roger was right back in the middle of the third grade.

"Oh, get out of here, Roger. Go stick your head in the fish tank."

Roger and his two buddies laughed hard. Roger leaned down and grinned right into Marsha's face. He smelled like waffles and maple syrup.

"Now, Marsha. Is that any way to talk to an old friend?" Roger patted Marsha on the back. "Did you wake up on the wrong side of bed, again?"

Marsha wiggled her shoulders until Roger pulled away his hand. She noticed his hand already had ink marks all over it. He had drawn little eyes on top of each knuckle.

Roger was so weird. He didn't belong in the third grade. He didn't belong on the

planet Earth. He should be in a large cage in the Highland Park Zoo with a STAND BACK, I BITE! sign in front.

"My, what a neat little desk you have there." Roger bent down and stuck his head right inside Marsha's desk like he was checking on pies in an oven. "Neat as a pin, all right."

"Get out of my desk before your cooties get inside," warned Marsha. She stretched out her neck, looking for her friends, Collette and Sarah. If they came over, Roger wouldn't be so rude. Roger saved his worst behavior for Marsha.

As soon as Marsha turned back, she saw Roger reach in his pockets. Before she could say a word, he tossed two handfuls of tiny wrinkled gum wrappers right in the middle of her desk. Little balls of red, yellow, and green wrappers, sparkling with tin foil, lay on top of her new books like bread crumbs.

"Now *that* looks more like your desk," hooted Roger. He patted the litter and gave Marsha one more whack on the back. "Welcome to the third grade, ape face!"

"Get away from me, Roger Friday!" Marsha slammed down her desktop so hard, Roger's fingertips almost snapped off. He started hopping up and down like he was on a hot black skillet.

"Oweeee! Oh geez . . ." Roger blew on his fingers and crossed his eyes.

"Oh, stop it, you're okay!" Marsha bit her lip. Roger really didn't *look* okay. In fact, he looked like his eyeballs were going to pop out of his head and roll across the floor. "Hey, I didn't mean to . . ." Marsha chewed on the end of her braid. Holy cow, what if Mrs. Byrnes walked in now? She would want to know who started trouble in Room 10. Marsha made a fist. Boy, oh, boy! If she hadn't already promised her parents she'd be good, she would poke Roger right in the nose and tell him to sit down and be quiet.

Roger's friends kept trying to pat Roger on the back. It was pretty hard to do since he kept hopping up and down.

"What happened?" Sarah and Collette ran over and stood by Marsha's desk. "What did you do to him, Marsha?"

"Nothing!" Marsha tugged at her bangs. She didn't do it on purpose. "His hand got in the way of me slamming my desk."

"Call 911 . . . I need a finger transplant!" hollered Roger. He twirled around and around the teacher's desk with his hand high in the air. "My whole hand is going to fall off."

"Oh it is *not!*" insisted Marsha. She ran up the aisle and tried to look at Roger's hand. It wasn't even bleeding. Roger always made a big deal about everything. He knew that she didn't mean to hurt him. She had just wanted him to leave her alone. That's all she had *ever* wanted. Roger Friday had been bugging her ever since the first grade, when he put a runover snake in her locker. This kid was a maniac!

"Children!"

The room got quiet fast, like traffic screeching to a halt. Of course, Roger was the only one *still* making a lot of noise. Marsha saw him grin when Mrs. Byrnes walked into the room. Then he scrunched up his face as if he was going to cry.

"I heard you all the way down the hall!" said Mrs. Byrnes. She flicked the lights on and off two times. "Take your seats."

They all ran back to their seats and tried to look good.

"Will somebody please tell me what is going on?" Mrs. Byrnes sat down in her chair and frowned. "What happened to you, Roger?"

Roger bit his lip. Marsha saw the way he was blinking his eyes. He was probably trying to squeeze out a tear. Oh, good grief! Now he was sniffing. What a faker!

"He's okay," said Marsha quickly. She stood up and took a step closer. She looked Roger right in the eye. Roger had to know that she didn't mean to hurt him. If he got her in trouble with Mrs. Byrnes, she would really be mad at him.

"Marsha slammed her desk on Roger's hand," offered Chester. He shoved his glasses up a notch and stood straighter, as if he were talking to the police. "I was sharpening my pencils at the time, and I heard them fighting. They fight a lot. In second grade, Miss Duffy had to — "

"Thank you, Chester. I get the picture." Mrs. Byrnes turned and frowned at Marsha. She looked so disappointed Marsha almost burst into tears. Boy, that Roger Friday was always getting her in trouble. Slamming his fingers in the desktop had been an accident.

"I think I better go for X rays," said Roger in a weak voice. "Gee, I hope I can still move my fingers. My mother was going to sign me up for piano lessons this year, and . . ."

Mrs. Byrnes walked over and bent and tested Roger's hand. "You seem okay. You'll be able to play the piano. But, why don't you go wash your hand, Roger? Your knuckles are staring at me."

Roger shook his hand. "Yeah, well, I guess I'm okay. But my thumb is really sore. I hope this doesn't hurt my basketball game. My team is counting on me."

Marsha groaned. Good grief! Roger made up lies and bragged about himself so much it wasn't even funny!

Mrs. Byrnes walked over to Marsha. "I'm

sure it was an accident. But, Marsha, wouldn't you like to apologize to Roger?"

"What?" sputtered Marsha. "Why? He owes *me* the apology, Mrs. Byrnes. I mean, I was minding my own business and he came up to me and started bothering me and . . ."

Mrs. Byrnes looked down through her glasses at Marsha. She was wearing her disappointed face again. "Is this how we want to start third grade?"

Marsha chewed on the inside of her cheek. Third grade was supposed to be perfect. But now she wasn't so sure. Since Roger was in her homeroom, maybe *quitting* the third grade would be the easiest thing to do. It would be the only way she would get away from Roger Friday.

"Marsha . . ." Mrs. Byrnes reached out and pulled Roger closer. Roger tried to look innocent and hurt. He held his arm out to his side like a broken wing.

"Can't we be friends, Marsha?" Roger asked in a sugar-coated voice. He smiled up at Mrs. Byrnes like that was what he wanted more than anything in the whole world.

Marsha wanted to poke Roger right in his smart alecky face. But she swallowed her temper and shook Roger's hand. She didn't do it because she wanted to be friends with him. She did it because she liked Mrs. Byrnes. She did it because she had promised her parents that third grade would be different.

Marsha stomped back to her seat. As long as Roger Friday was in the same classroom, third grade would *never* be different. There was only one way to have a fresh start at Sacred Heart Elementary. And that meant getting rid of Roger Friday!

Chapter
<u>Two</u>

Mrs. Byrnes didn't act mad at Marsha, but the first day of third grade was still ruined. Spoiled by mean old Roger Friday. Marsha tried very hard in spelling to print all of her words neatly. They looked like a typewriter had done them. In science Roger turned around twice to see what Marsha was doing. Twice Marsha had covered up her work and kicked the back of Roger's seat. Roger was too dumb to know when someone didn't want to talk to him. Marsha never wanted to talk to Roger again. Never in her whole life.

Staying mad at someone was hard work.

By lunchtime, Marsha had a giant headache. By the time she squeezed in between Collette and Sarah at the cafeteria table, she was ready to go home. But if she went home, her mother would be waiting at the door, a big smile on her face. "How was the first day of school, Marsha?" she would ask. "Does Mrs. Byrnes think you are the best little girl in her class?" Marsha sighed. Her poor mother would stop smiling the moment she heard that Marsha was the first person in the third grade to get yelled at by Mrs. Byrnes. Marsha slammed down her lunch bag; she didn't even open it. She wasn't a bit hungry. She would probably never eat again, now that Mrs. Byrnes had forced her to shake hands with Roger Friday in front of the whole class. Marsha shuddered and wiped her hand off on her uniform. Maybe she should go get a shot in case Roger was contagious.

Collette set a pretzel down in front of Marsha and Sarah. "Here, guys. A little treat. Boy, the morning went so fast. Third grade is a lot of fun. I can hardly wait for the spelling bee after lunch." Collette took a bite of her sandwich. "Hurry up and eat, Marsha, so we can go outside and play."

Marsha sighed. She pushed her lunch bag away and leaned both elbows on the table. "I'm not hungry. I don't even feel like going outside."

"Marsha!" Sarah pushed Marsha's lunch bag back in front of her. "I heard we got new playground balls. Let's hurry and play four square." She patted Marsha on the back. "Don't let Roger get you upset."

Marsha sat up and shook back her dark hair. "Easy for you to say. He doesn't bother you two, just me."

Collette giggled. "Remember in first grade when he told the substitute he was your twin brother?"

Sarah laughed. "And remember last year when Roger taped that sign on your back. 'Kiss me quick. I'm really a frog!'?"

Collette and Sarah both giggled.

Marsha frowned. It made her mad to hear her two best friends laughing about the terrible things that Roger Friday did to her.

Why did everyone think Roger was so funny? He wasn't. Not one bit of him was funny. In fact, there was a screw loose in his head. Maybe two screws.

Collette leaned over and opened Marsha's lunch bag. She pulled out a package of cheese crackers. "I know he bugs you, Marsha. But if you just ignore him, he'll stop. My little brothers do the same stuff to me."

"Yeah, but at least you can tell your mother, and she can put them in their rooms."

Collette laughed. "Not always. Stevie would never get *out* of his room if he got punished for everything."

Marsha and Collette both started to laugh. Stevie was only two years old and got in lots of trouble. But even Stevie wasn't as bad as Roger. Stevie did little kid stuff like flushing his socks down the toilet. Marsha was sure that Roger must stay up late at night, just thinking of terrible things to do to get her in trouble. She would take a *thousand* Stevie Murphys before she would take one Roger Friday.

Marsha glanced down the table. There was Roger with his two buddies, Michael and Timmy. They were laughing with their mouths open so you could see the chewed-up food.

"Sister Mary Elizabeth should have a special room for people like Roger," said Marsha. "A room with padded walls and no windows."

Sarah and Collette started to laugh. Collette reached across and took one of Marsha's crackers. "Start eating, Marsha. Hey, isn't it exciting about the student teacher coming today?"

Marsha nodded. "Miss Murtland . . . that's such a pretty name. I hope she looks like the student teacher the sixth-graders had last year. She had a red braid all the way down her back."

"And she used to read stories to the class all the time," added Sarah. "Remember how she never ate lunch in the teachers' room? She took turns eating with all the sixth-graders."

Marsha took a big bite of her bologna

sandwich. Student teachers were a lot of fun. Last year the fourth grade had one named Miss Ramsey. But she let the kids call her Miss Judith. At lunchtime she even let the girls comb her hair. Maybe Miss Murtland would let Marsha comb her hair. Maybe Miss Murtland would find a way to keep Roger from bothering her.

Collette bent down and grinned at Marsha. "Well, it's nice to see you smiling again, Marsha."

"I was just thinking about Miss Murtland. I like her already."

"Me, too," said Sarah. "Mrs. Byrnes said we get to keep her for six whole weeks."

"That's a long time," agreed Collette. "I hope she eats lunch with us first. I'll bring four pretzels tomorrow. One for Miss Murtland."

Marsha took another bite of her sandwich, then another. She wanted to finish her lunch fast. After recess she would meet Miss Murtland. Mrs. Byrnes had told Room 10 that Miss Murtland was just about to finish college and was working on a special paper.

Third grade was very lucky to get some-body as special as Miss Murtland. She had spent four years learning all about teaching kids. Marsha smiled. She felt lucky all right. Maybe Miss Murtland had taken a class that told teachers what to do about rude trou-blemakers, like Roger. Maybe Miss Murt-land would send him back to the second grade.

Chapter Three

After recess, Mrs. Byrnes let everyone get a drink at the fountain. Marsha took a quick sip. She couldn't wait to get inside to meet the new student teacher. As soon as she walked in, she saw her. Miss Murtland was beautiful. She had brown curly hair and big silver earrings. She was smiling at the apple bulletin board. Maybe she was trying to memorize everyone's name.

Marsha slid into her seat. She licked her fingers and tried to smash down her bangs. Then she sat up very straight and folded her hands.

When everyone was back in the room,

Mrs. Byrnes closed the door. Miss Murtland stopped looking at the apples and walked to the front of the room. Her high heels made a nice *click, click, click, click* as she walked. Her silver bracelets jingled and her earrings swung back and forth.

Mrs. Byrnes smiled and held out her hand toward Miss Murtland. "Class, I would like to introduce your new student teacher, Miss Murtland." Mrs. Byrnes took a step back. Miss Murtland took a step forward. She nodded her head and smiled.

Miss Murtland was so pretty. She looked just like Wendy Dixon, the weather girl on channel four.

Marsha started to clap.

"Marsha," said Mrs. Byrnes softly. She raised both eyebrows. Marsha looked around the room. No one else had clapped. She put her hands down on her lap. Maybe you weren't supposed to clap for student teachers. Even if they were as pretty as Miss Murtland.

Roger turned around and pointed his pencil right into Marsha's face. "This isn't a game show, birdbrain."

Marsha leaned back in her seat and looked away. She didn't want to look at his rude face. She had to be patient. Any minute now Miss Murtland would ask the class for suggestions. Marsha would raise her hand. "Yes, Marsha, dear?" Miss Murtland would say. Maybe she would hurry down the aisle and put her arm, with all the dancing silver bracelets on it, right on Marsha's shoulder.

"I think we should rearrange our desks, Miss Murtland," Marsha would say loudly. "We should put Roger's desk out in the hall by the lost-and-found box."

"Marvelous idea, Marsha!" Miss Murtland would agree. Maybe she would slide one of her thin bracelets off and leave it on Marsha's desk. It could be her way of saying, "You're my favorite student already."

"Marsha! Marsha Cessano!"

Marsha jumped in her seat. Mrs. Byrnes was standing by her desk. "Why is your hand up, Marsha? Do you have a question?"

Marsha put her hand down. "Yes, I mean, no . . . but . . . if Miss Murtland wants to rearrange desks, I'll be glad to help."

Several children started to laugh. Roger turned around and crossed his eyes. Marsha could feel her face go red. She was glad that Sarah and Collette weren't laughing. Miss Murtland wasn't laughing, either. In the front of the room, Miss Murtland was writing her name on the blackboard:

Miss Murtland

Marsha smiled again. Miss Murtland wrote cursive beautifully. She crossed her "t" very carefully. It was perfectly level. Miss Murtland made a soft tap with the chalk as she dotted the i. Marsha picked up her pencil, wishing she had an i to dot or a t to cross in her name. If she did, she would have done it just the way Miss Murtland did.

Miss Murtland turned from the board and smiled. Marsha smiled back automatically. Marsha always smiled when she listened to Wendy Dixon do the weather report. Marsha wanted to do the weather when she grew up. Wendy would only stop smiling if she had to report a tornado watch or a flood.

"Good afternoon. It's so nice to be here," said Miss Murtland. "Y'all sure have a lovely school." Marsha felt like clapping again. Her teacher was from the South! Just like Scarlett O'Hara in *Gone With the Wind*.

Gone With the Wind was Marsha's very favorite film. She had seen the movie at least
five times with her Gramma Hughes. All
five times she and Gramma had cried at the
end. Once Marsha had cried so hard she
choked on her popcorn.

"Scarlett's temper sure got her in lots of
trouble," Gramma would always say, wip-
ing at her own eyes. "Let that be a lesson
to you, Marsha. Don't let your temper go
wild."

Marsha leaned back in her seat. She
wouldn't have to worry about her temper
once Roger Friday left the third grade. She
could hardly wait till Miss Murtland found
a way to get rid of him.

" . . . and since I am working on my
paper, I really do need your help. Does it
sound like something y'all might enjoy?"

Marsha sat up straighter, looking around
the room. Oh no, what had she missed? Did
Miss Murtland already ask for helpers? Had
Marsha missed out on a chance to volunteer?

Marsha raised her hand. "I'll enjoy it!"

She was sure that whatever Miss Murtland had suggested, she would like it.

Mrs. Byrnes smiled at Marsha. "Let's let Miss Murtland finish."

Miss Murtland sat on the edge of Sarah's desk. Marsha wished she sat in the front row so Miss Murtland would sit on *her* desk.

"I want to give each of you a buddy to work very closely with for the next few weeks. You will correct each other's homework, work together on a book report, and sit with each other on field trips." Miss Murtland smiled at Mrs. Byrnes. "I hear y'all get to visit Heinz and watch them make ketchup."

Marsha leaned forward. This buddy system sounded fun. Maybe Miss Murtland would let Sarah and Collette both be buddies with her.

Miss Murtland turned around and picked up a piece of paper. "Now Mrs. Byrnes sent me a class list several weeks ago and I have already picked a buddy for you."

Marsha crossed her fingers. "Oh, please

let me get either Sarah or Collette," she prayed.

"To make this as fair as possible," said Miss Murtland with a smile, "I am going to buddy y'all up alphabetically."

Marsha frowned. Phooey. Sarah's last name started with an M and so did Collette's. The two of them would be together. Marsha's last name started with a C.

As Miss Murtland started to read the buddy list aloud, Marsha looked around the room. Last year she was always with Billy Douglas, since nobody else had a last name starting with a C.

"Sally Alexander and Molly Andrews," read Miss Murtland. Sally and Molly both clapped their hands and grinned at each other.

Marsha turned in her seat, searching for Billy. Working with him wouldn't be too bad. He was very smart and kind of funny. At least he wasn't a pain in the neck like Roger Friday.

"Carrie Beeker and Michelle Bowling," continued Miss Murtland.

Marsha stretched her neck and searched the front row. Where was Billy anyway?

"Marsha Cessano and Billy Douglas," said Miss Murtland.

Mrs. Byrnes pushed up her glasses. She leaned over and checked Miss Murtland's list. She whispered something to Miss Murtland. Miss Murtland made some marks on her paper with her pencil. Marsha leaned forward. What was wrong?

Miss Murtland looked up and smiled. "Mrs. Byrnes just told me that Billy Douglas moved to Florida over the summer. So, now Marsha Cessano will now be working with. . . ." Miss Murtland looked down at her paper. "With her new buddy, Roger Friday."

"What?" cried Marsha.

Miss Murtland and Mrs. Byrnes both looked surprised. Roger turned around and wiggled his eyebrows up and down. "Yo! Buddy," he said.

Marsha leaned back in her seat. She felt dizzy. She felt weak. She felt like Miss Murtland had just tossed a fifty-pound rock on her stomach. There had to be some sort of mistake. She couldn't work with Roger Friday.

"Is everything all right, Marsha?" Miss Murtland stood up and smiled at Marsha. "You are going to help me with my paper, aren't you?"

Marsha tried to swallow the big lump in her throat. She nodded. "Yes."

Miss Murtland sat back down and finished reading the rest of the list. Sarah and Collette did get to be together. They were so lucky.

Marsha put her head down on her desk. She was so unlucky. Why couldn't *Roger* have moved to Florida over the summer instead of Billy Douglas?

Why was third grade so unfair?

Chapter
Four

When the dismissal bell finally rang, Marsha was the first one in line for the bus. She didn't go over and talk to Miss Murtland with Collette and Sarah. She was in such a bad mood, she didn't want to talk to anyone. She wanted to go home and think. She had to come up with a plan. A plan to get rid of Roger. If he were kicked out of the third grade, Marsha would be buddies with someone normal like Shannon Gaines or William Gilmore. Anyone but Roger!

Marsha was quiet on the bus ride home. She barely talked to Collette.

"I feel so bad for you, Marsha," said Collette. She patted Marsha gently on the arm. "I sure wish your last name was Miller or McBride so you could have gotten Sarah or me for a partner."

Marsha nodded. It was too late now. She was a Cessano and Roger was a Friday. Unless someone with a last name starting with D or E transferred into Sacred Heart, she would be spending the rest of her life with Roger Friday. Marsha shuddered. What a horrible thought. Maybe she could ask her parents to change their last name. Nothing too different. They could just add one letter. One little letter would change Cessano into L'Cessano. Marsha smiled. It sounded good. And best of all, Miss Murtland would change the list. Marsha could be buddies with Mary Lou Lennard.

If only her parents would go along with it. They were usually pretty nice to her. Very nice in fact. She was probably the only third-grader at Sacred Heart who had a color television in her room.

But what if they didn't like the idea of changing their last name? They were pretty old, almost forty. People that old didn't like a whole lot of changes.

Marsha's feet practically dragged as she walked up her front steps. She felt like she had cement inside her brown loafers. Her parents just had to say yes to her plan. Working with Roger was bad for her health. She already felt weaker. Marsha stopped. Maybe that was a way out. Her mother could write a note to Miss Murtland explaining that her daughter was allergic to Roger Friday. Any close contact with Roger could cause sneezing, headaches, and possibly throwing up.

Marsha smiled. Miss Murtland wouldn't want that. For the first time in hours, Marsha began to feel like her old self. Actually, she was feeling a lot like Scarlett O'Hara in *Gone With the Wind*. Scarlett had lots of problems. But she always managed to find a way out of them. She never gave up. Marsha had two plans now. Surely her parents would say yes to at least one of them.

"I'm home, Mom!" called out Marsha.

She walked across the hall and into the kitchen. It smelled like cookies.

Mrs. Cessano looked up from her crossword puzzle book. "How was your first day, honey?"

Marsha dropped her book bag and slid into the chair. Her mother always had a snack waiting for her. Today, it was warm oatmeal cookies and apple cider. "Fine. Mrs. Byrnes is real nice. Guess what? We got a new student teacher. Mom, she is *so* pretty. Her name is Miss Murtland. She looks just like Wendy Dixon and she talks just like Scarlett O'Hara."

Mrs. Cessano laughed. "Wow, that's a nice combination."

Marsha took a long drink of cider. She set down her glass and looked across the table at her mother. "The day was pretty okay. Except for one thing."

Mrs. Cessano set down her pencil. She looked worried. "What is the one thing?"

"Roger Friday."

Mrs. Cessano frowned. "Roger is not a *thing,* Marsha."

"He is, Mom. You don't know him like I do. His mother probably found him under a rock one day."

Mrs. Cessano stood up and poured herself a glass of cider. "That's not funny, Marsha. Now, you promised Daddy and me this morning that you were going to make a fresh start."

Marsha nodded. "I know. I am. You should see how neat my desk is. I didn't talk in class. I was the first one to hand in a math paper. . . ."

Mrs. Cessano smiled. "Wonderful. And I'm sure, *this year*, you are going to find a way to deal with Roger Friday. You have been at war with that little boy for two years."

Marsha set down her cookie. "I know. In fact, I already have a plan. Two plans. You can pick the one you like best."

Mrs. Cessano sat down and reached across the table. She patted Marsha's hand. "Good girl. Wait till your father hears this. He was getting very tired of you and Roger fighting all the time."

Marsha smiled back. "Me, too. And I don't want Miss Murtland to see one fight. So that's why I have my plans."

Mrs. Cessano leaned forward. Marsha liked that about being an only child. Her parents always wanted to hear what she had to say, every word. "Go ahead, Marsha. I'm all ears."

Marsha drew in a deep breath. "Well, today Miss Murtland told us about this buddy project of hers. She is making us work with another person as a team. We have to sit with them on field trips, check each other's papers, do a book report together . . ."

Mrs. Cessano looked interested. "It must be a research study of some sort."

Marsha shrugged. "I guess. I think she wants to see if we get better marks on our papers. Collette and Sarah get to work together."

Mrs. Cessano nodded. "Sounds interesting. Who is your buddy?"

Marsha took a deep breath. "Roger Friday."

"Roger Friday?" Mrs. Cessano broke into

a huge smile. "Well, I guess the two of you *will* stop fighting then. Your father and I always thought you and Roger would get along fine once you got to know each other."

Marsha choked on her apple cider. "No, we will fight even more, Mom. That's why I came up with my plans."

Mrs. Cessano stopped smiling. "Tell me about your plans."

Marsha smiled. She would tell her mother about the name change first. That was her favorite. "Well, we both know I can't work with Roger. We both know that he's nuts, Mom. We both know that he gets me in trouble all the time. We both know — "

"What is your plan, Marsha?" Her mother didn't look at all happy. She looked like she already hated the plan.

"Well," said Marsha brightly. "I thought that you could write Miss Murtland a note tonight. Tell her that we changed our last name over the summer . . ."

"What?"

"Tell her that we thought L'Cessano

35

sounded fancier and . . ." Marsha saw her mother's frown and started talking faster. "And that you would like me to use my new last name and work with Mary Lou Lennard."

Mrs. Cessano shook her head. She kept shaking it for about fifty shakes. Any minute now her head would fall off and roll across the table. "No, no, no! We are not going to change our last name. Besides, I *like* Roger. There is nothing wrong with the boy."

Marsha felt tears stinging. How could her mother say that? Of course there was some-thing *wrong* with Roger Friday. The kid was nuts! He wasn't happy unless he was getting Marsha into trouble.

Mrs. Cessano reached across the table and took Marsha's hand. "We are *not* changing our last name, Marsha. Now would you like to tell me about your second plan? I hope it's better than the first."

Marsha felt like taking back her hand. Didn't her mother realize that working with Roger was worse than eating liver or getting booster shots?

"You won't like my second plan, either." Marsha tried to sound as sad as she could. Her mother hated to see her sad. Any minute now she would get up and pull Marsha on her lap. Any minute now she would say, "Oh, all right, Marsha. Of course we will change our last name if it will make you happy."

But Mrs. Cessano just leaned back in her chair and sighed. "Marsha, I think that third grade is a good time for you to do a little growing up."

Marsha sniffed loudly. Oh, great. Now even her very own mother was being mean to her.

"I think working with Roger is the perfect way to get to know him better."

"I don't *want* to get to know him better," said Marsha. "I know him well enough to know that I don't like him. I bet I'm allergic to him. I'll break out in huge spots. Is that what you want?"

Mrs. Cessano smiled and patted Marsha's hand. "Give the kid a chance. You said you wanted third grade to be a fresh start."

Marsha sighed. It wouldn't do any good to talk to her mother about this. Her mother wanted her to be fair and good and kind. Marsha sighed. Too bad she didn't have some brothers or sisters around so they could be those things.

There was only one thing Marsha wanted to be right now. She wanted to be far, far away from Roger Friday.

Chapter
<u>Five</u>

Early the next morning, Marsha cornered Collette and Sarah by the water fountain. "I want you to be the first to know," Marsha announced. "Today is the first day of the rest of my life!"

Collette groaned. "Oh, brother, Marsha. You sound like a greeting card."

"People who write greeting cards end up on talk shows," insisted Marsha.

"Whatever," laughed Sarah. "Come on or we'll all be late."

Marsha hurried ahead, down the hall. "I can't ever be late again." She shifted her book bag and reached to open her locker.

She stopped. A note was taped to it.

Roses are red
violets are blue
no bud-dy in school
is as ugly as
you!

"Oh, that dumb old Roger Friday!" exploded Marsha. She ripped the note off her locker and wrinkled it up. After she rolled it into a tight ball, she jumped up and down on it.

"What's wrong, Marsha?" asked Collette. "What are you doing?"

"Hey, looks like Marsha ate Mexican jumping beans for breakfast again," laughed Roger from the door. "Higher, Marsha, higher."

Marsha stopped jumping. She gave Roger a mean look and picked up the smashed paper. "I know you wrote this, Roger. If we weren't in school I would shove this paper right down your skinny throat!"

Roger's eyes flew open. He put both of his hands around his neck and gagged. "No, please, no, Marsha! Help, help!"

Marsha tossed the note inside her locker and slammed the door. When she looked up, Miss Murtland was patting Roger on the back. "Are you all right, sugar? What's wrong?"

Roger's face flooded red. He took his hands away from his throat. "I . . . I just swallowed a bug, that's all."

Miss Murtland gave him one final pat and smiled. "You all better hurry now. The bell is about to ring."

As soon as Miss Murtland went inside, Marsha stomped over to Roger. "Listen, bug-brain. I don't want any more notes from you, okay? In fact, do us both a favor and stay far, far away from me."

Roger grinned. "But you're my buddy."

Marsha closed her eyes and made a fist. "And don't call me your buddy. I am not your buddy. I will never *be* your buddy, understand?"

Roger flattened himself against the lockers. He took a big swallow and nodded his head. "Yes, sir. Aye, aye, Captain . . . anything you say, Sarge!"

Marsha growled and walked quickly into the classroom. Roger was worse than ever. He had probably stayed up till midnight planning all sorts of awful things to spring today.

"Just ignore him, Marsha," suggested Collette. "He'll stop once class starts."

Marsha slid into her seat and sighed. She really hoped so. The thought of being with Roger for weeks and weeks made her sick to her stomach. It wasn't fair. Why couldn't her last name have been Zannyzoo-zoo?

Marsha lifted the lid of her desk. She wanted to make sure it was still as neat as yesterday. Her parents were so proud of her. Last night after dinner her father had given her a brand-new pen and pencil set. A big

"M" was engraved on both the pen and pencil. Marsha reached into her pocket and took them out. They would look great inside her desk.

"Hey, what happened to those gum wrappers I gave you yesterday?" asked Roger. His head was right next to her cheek. His whole head seemed warm, like a huge baked potato.

"Get away from me," snapped Marsha. She put her pen and pencil inside and carefully closed her desk. She kept her eyes on Roger's fat fingers the whole time. She didn't want Roger to pretend he was hurt again.

"Boy, you sure aren't a morning person, are you?" asked Roger. He sat down in his seat, turned around, and grinned at Marsha. "But I am, Marsha. That's the neat thing about having a buddy. You and I are good together because we are opposites. I am cheerful, you are a grouch. I am smart and you are dumb. I am — "

Marsha leaned forward. "You are a big pain in the neck, Roger Friday. Now turn around. Why don't you hold your breath until you explode?"

Roger's cheeks got pink. Next the tips of his ears got a little red. But finally, he turned around.

Marsha drew in a deep breath. She hated it when she let her temper go wild. Scarlett O'Hara let her temper go wild the whole way through *Gone With the Wind*. Scarlett lied, cheated, and made lots of people mad. Marsha frowned. Scarlett was the prettiest movie star she had ever seen. But even pretty movie stars ended up in trouble by letting their tempers go wild.

Marsha stared at the back of Roger's head. From the back, he almost looked normal. She looked around the room. Everyone was putting away books or sharpening pencils. Miss Murtland was laughing and sipping coffee from a big mug. Marsha smiled. She could hardly wait for the day to start. Miss Murtland was going to teach them English and spelling today, all by herself. Third grade was going to be wonderful.

"Just a few more minutes before the bell," reminded Mrs. Byrnes.

Marsha looked back at Roger's neck. Third grade was not going to be wonderful though, if she was going to fight with Roger every day. Maybe she should tell Roger the war between them should stop. It should stop before Miss Murtland found out. It should stop before it got any worse.

Marsha reached out to tap Roger on the back. The thought of actually saying she was sorry to someone as rude as Roger was hard. The bell was going to ring any minute. She stood up and walked to the windows. Maybe if she just took a few deep breaths, it would be easier. She should think about all the good reasons she should try to be friends with Roger. First of all, her parents would be so happy. They loved it when she said she was sorry to people. Her mother said saying you were sorry was a sign of a good heart.

Marsha smiled. She liked the sound of having a good heart. Too bad no one had talked to Scarlett O'Hara about having a good heart. She never had a chance to tame her wild temper.

Marsha looked out across the wide green lawn of Sacred Heart Elementary. The principal, Sister Mary Elizabeth, Mrs. Byrnes, and especially Miss Murtland would all be proud of her for trying to be friends with Roger. Marsha looked over at Miss Murtland. She would do it. She would march over right now and call off the war.

As soon as Marsha slid back into her seat, the morning bell rang. She bent across to tap Roger on the back. The sooner she got this over with, the better. Mrs. Byrnes flashed the lights on and off. That meant no talking while Sister Mary Elizabeth got ready to read morning prayers over the PA system. Marsha carefully opened her desk and reached for her new pen. She would scribble Roger a quick note . . . *Dear Roger, I won't bug you anymore if you won't bug me* . . . That would be a good start. Marsha grinned. Her parents were going to be so excited. They would probably take her out to dinner to celebrate or maybe to a movie or. . . .

Marsha opened her desk higher. She bent down and moved her tablet, then her Magic Marker box. Where was her new pen and pencil set? She had just put it in here a minute ago.

Marsha ruffled quickly through her desk. Where could they be? She stuck her head inside and knocked over two neat stacks of books. Somebody must have stolen her new pen and pencil set. Marsha let out a small cry and stood up. She emptied her red notebook upside down. Papers and lunch tickets floated slowly to the floor. But no pen fell out. No pencil with a big "M."

Marsha reached in and used both hands. She tossed books and papers around like a giant salad. Her desk was a total mess but she didn't care. She had to find her new pen and pencil set. She had been planning to keep it for the rest of her whole life.

"Marsha, what are you doing?" called out Mrs. Byrnes from the front of the room. "Prayers are about to start."

Marsha slammed down the desk lid and felt tears stinging her eyes. "I can't find my pen and pencil set."

Roger just laughed. "Oh, go buy a box of CrackerJack and get yourself another one." He shook his head at the papers spilling out of Marsha's desk. "Holy cow, what a mess!" Roger leaned far away from her papers, acting as if they were a raging fire.

"What's wrong?" Mrs. Byrnes asked. She hurried quickly down the aisle.

"I can't find my pen and pencil set," cried Marsha.

Roger tapped Marsha's desktop. "What are you, a broken record?"

Over the PA Sister Mary Elizabeth started to wish everyone a good morning. Mrs. Byrnes put her arm around Marsha and put her finger to her lips with the other hand. No one was allowed to talk during morning prayers.

Marsha tried to pay attention. She even closed her eyes and prayed that her pen and pencil set would be found soon. In the middle of the "Our Father" prayer Marsha glanced over at Roger. Roger had seen her pen and pencil. In fact . . . in fact, he had been the *only one* to see them.

Sister Mary Elizabeth had barely finished the "Our Father" when Marsha tugged on Mrs. Byrnes's sleeve. "Roger stole my pen and pencil, Mrs. Byrnes. I just know it."

Everyone looked shocked, especially Roger. His mouth fell open and his cheeks got all spotty red.

"No way!" he shouted.

Marsha nodded her head and crossed her arms. Just wait till Mrs. Byrnes and Miss Murtland opened his desk. Just wait till all of Room 10 saw the shiny pen and pencil with the fancy "M." Maybe then Roger would get thrown out of school for good. Marsha smiled, glad the truth was finally out. Glad that she didn't have to say she was sorry to rude Roger Friday. Glad that Roger was finally going to get kicked out of third grade.

Chapter Six

"Just look inside his messy old desk if you don't believe me," Marsha said loudly. Wait till Miss Murtland looked inside. Mrs. Byrnes would drag Roger down to the office so fast, his feet wouldn't touch the floor.

Before Mrs. Byrnes could even take a step closer, Roger opened his desk. Marsha leaned closer. Kids got out of their seats and peered inside.

Roger's desk was as neat as a pin. His books were arranged smallest to biggest. His pencils were bound together with a fat, red rubber band.

Mrs. Byrnes lifted up books and tablets. She moved everything around and around.

"Your pen and pencil set is not inside Roger's desk. You made a mistake, Marsha."

Everyone looked up at Marsha. Lots of kids were frowning. Miss Murtland raised one eyebrow and said, "Oh my," in a soft, disappointed voice.

"Marsha, I don't see your pen and pencil set in Roger's desk," said Mrs. Byrnes. "You must be very sure before you say somebody stole something from you."

Roger held out both hands. "Yeah, I didn't take your rinky-dink pen or pencil." Roger bent down and yanked off his tennis shoe. "You want to search my socks or something, Marsha?"

A few kids laughed. Marsha's cheeks felt like hot coals. Her pen and pencil set had to be somewhere in Roger's desk. He had to be the one who took it.

"Maybe we should all pair off with our buddies and help Marsha find her pen and pencil set," suggested Miss Murtland. "We have a few minutes before it's time to line up for gym class."

Marsha felt like crying. Why would she want to pair up with Roger? Roger was the one who took the pen and pencil set.

Pretty soon everyone was looking for the pen and pencil set. Most of the kids were just fooling around and looking in silly places. Michael and Michelle looked in the fish tank. Erin and Vanessa looked on top of the globe.

"So why don't we look in your desk?" said Roger. He had both hands shoved deep in his pockets. He looked pretty mad.

"It's not in *my* desk," said Marsha. She looked over at Roger's desk.

Roger let out a deep breath. Then he lifted his desktop. "Go ahead and look again. I don't have anything to hide."

"Of course you don't." Miss Murtland seemed to have jumped out of nowhere. She smiled at Roger and Marsha. "Now why don't we all work together? That would be real nice."

Marsha watched Miss Murtland as she talked. Miss Murtland had the whitest teeth she had ever seen. They looked like the teeth on Marsha's very expensive Japanese doll with the yellow fan.

"Okay," said Marsha. "I'll look in your desk, Roger, and you look in my desk."

Miss Murtland clapped her hands like the case had already been solved. "There you go."

Marsha slid into Roger's seat and lifted his desktop. Boy, did it feel funny to be sitting in Roger Friday's seat. She looked at the red rabbit's foot in the corner of his desk. It had a silver key on it. Marsha glanced across her shoulder. Did Roger have to watch himself after school?

Marsha moved a few books around. But she was only trying to look like she was searching his desk. It was so neat inside you could tell right away that her beautiful pen and pencil set wasn't inside.

But if Roger hadn't taken it, who had?

"Here it is!"

Marsha spun around and watched as

Roger held up the silver pen and pencil. Lots of kids started to clap. Roger made a small bow. Miss Murtland patted him on the back.

"Where were they?" asked Marsha. How could Roger have found them so soon, anyway? He probably had them in his pocket the whole time.

"They were right in your desk," said Roger. He still looked kind of mad. "They were inside your marker box."

"Roger just opened the box and there they were," said Miss Murtland.

Marsha's face flooded red. Oh my gosh! She *had* put them there. She was trying to be so neat that she. . . .

"Oh, brother," said Michael.

"Boy, was Marsha wrong," added Lorraine. "All that looking for nothing."

Mrs. Byrnes flashed the lights on and off. "Okay, class. Line up for gym."

Marsha held out her hand for the pen and pencil. "Sorry, Roger," she said softly.

But Roger just ignored her hand. He set the pen and pencil down on her desk and walked away. He didn't even look at her as he walked past to get in line.

Marsha felt terrible. She didn't even say a word when the silver pencil, and then the pen, rolled off her desktop and clattered to the floor.

Chapter
<u>Seven</u>

Marsha loved gym. It was her favorite class. But not today. She felt terrible. She had told the whole class Roger had stolen her pen and pencil set. Now the inside of her stomach felt jumpy, as if dozens of grasshoppers were dancing. It was all Roger's fault. If he had yelled back at her in homeroom, she wouldn't be feeling so guilty now. He *should* have said, "I didn't take your crummy pen and pencil set. You're a real jerk for saying I did." But he hadn't said a mean word back. He just stood there looking sad.

Marsha sighed. Having Roger looking

sad was even worse than having him mad. At least she could *ignore* him when he was just mad. Besides, she had been wrong. Marsha frowned. Boy, she *hated* being wrong. Especially about Roger. She should just go over and tell Roger she was really, truly sorry. But the thought of that gave Marsha a headache. Maybe if she said it real fast, the awful feeling inside her stomach would go away, and —

"Hey, wake up, Marsha!"

A red kickball flew past Marsha's left ear. She gave a quick hop backward.

"Marsha!" yelled Sarah. "Why didn't you catch it? Vanessa would have been out!"

Marsha looked up. The whole gym class was staring at her. Miss Poplin, the gym teacher, raised one eyebrow. "One point for the blue team."

Marsha bit her lip. She rubbed her hands together and tried to look alert. She always got A's in gym class. If she hadn't been thinking about dumb Roger Friday she would have caught that ball.

"One point for the good guys!" shouted out Roger. He licked his finger and held it high in the air. "Lucky for us Marsha was asleep on the job." The blue team laughed. No one on the red team laughed. Some of the kids from the red team turned around to frown at Marsha.

Marsha shook back her hair. So okay, she *hadn't* been paying attention. A person couldn't pay attention every second of her life, could she? She'd catch the next ball, even if she had to jump four feet into the air to get it. Let's see how hard Roger Friday would laugh then.

The rest of the game went fast. After thirty minutes, the score was still one–zip, and the red team had the score of zip. Marsha felt terrible, knowing she had let the blue team score. If the blue team won by only one point, everyone would blame her. Roger would probably write it on the playground with black shoe polish. Maybe he would rent an airplane to skywrite the score all over Pittsburgh.

Joel stepped up to home plate. Collette carefully rolled the ball toward him. With a mighty kick, Joel shot the ball straight over Collette's head. The ball headed out toward second. Jennifer and Matt both charged for it, their arms outstretched.

"I've got it," called out Matt.

"It's mine," Jennifer shouted.

The ball bounced hard in the middle of them both. The blue team hopped up and down and started laughing and shouting. Roger held up both arms and danced around. Joel was safe at first.

"Five more minutes," reminded Miss Poplin, checking her watch. "There's still time to even out the score. The game isn't over yet."

Roger walked slowly up to home plate, swinging his arms and smiling. He stretched his muscles and scratched his chin. He pretended he was chewing tobacco, like a major league player. Even Miss Poplin smiled at him. Marsha frowned. That was the trouble with Roger. He did really show-offy things, and teachers smiled. Marsha tugged on her bangs and waited for Roger to kick the ball. At least he didn't look sad anymore. Roger was the type who never stayed mad or sad about anything. That was one nice thing about him. Maybe the only nice thing.

Collette rolled the ball down the floor. Roger ran up and kicked. He missed, almost tripping on the side of the ball. "Whoa, what a fast pitch, Collette!"

"Nice try, Roger!" laughed Michael from second base. "Play kickball much?"

Miss Poplin gave a slight frown. She didn't like it when kids in her gym class acted like bad sports.

For the second pitch, Collette shot the ball down even faster. It went far to the left of home plate, but Roger hopped over and kicked it anyway. It was foul.

Marsha glanced at the clock above the bleachers. Only a few minutes left. The blue team already had two outs. If they got Roger out, there might be enough time for the red team to get another turn up. Leroy Merkle would be up next and he was a good player. He always kicked doubles. Then Marsha would be up. She could easily kick in the winning run. The red team would charge out onto the field to pick her up. Maybe they would carry her out into the hall on their shoulders.

"Come on, Collette, strike the loser out!" Marsha clamped her hand over her mouth. Holy cow, she didn't mean to say that out loud. Her mouth must have been open and the words just shot out!

Miss Poplin gave a short blast. She tapped her whistle on her hand and frowned at Marsha. "I want good sports in my class, Marsha."

Roger looked over at Marsha and smiled. It was a real smart-alecky smile. Then he turned around and looked at the clock. It was almost time for the bell to ring. Roger put his hands together and called for a time out.

"You can't have time out in gym class, Roger!" cried Marsha. "Just hurry up and kick the ball so we can tag you out!"

Both teams turned to stare at Miss Poplin. Miss Poplin looked up at the clock. "What's wrong, Roger? We really are running out of time."

Roger bent down and quickly untied and retied his shoes. "My shoelaces were loose. And since I'm planning to kick a home run, I want to make sure I can run fast."

Marsha groaned. Roger was just trying to waste time, that's all.

Collette rolled a perfect pitch down the gym floor. It was heading straight for home plate. Roger took a running step forward and whacked the ball high across everyone's head. Even Amon, the tallest kid in the class, couldn't hop high enough to touch it.

"Catch it!" screamed Marsha.

The ball sailed toward the bleachers by third base and bounced hard against the wall. Then it rolled ninety miles an hour across the floor. Half the red team left their positions and raced after the ball. Marsha stood stock still. She watched Roger run like a wild rabbit past second and third base. She groaned as he slid across home plate.

Roger got up and leaped high into the air. He was acting as if he had single-handedly won the World Series. Roger dusted off both knees, then his elbows, like he was covered with grass and dirt. Boy, that kid was always showing off.

Miss Poplin grinned and patted Roger's head. When the bell rang, everyone ran to line up. Lots of kids crowded around Roger to pound him on the back.

Marsha walked slowly across the floor. Roger got to feel like a hero, not her. Now he got to walk around all day feeling important. It wasn't fair. If Roger hadn't taken so much time, then the red team would have had a chance to be up. Then Marsha would have made the winning run and everyone would be crowded around her.

"Good game, Rog," called out kids from both teams. Miss Poplin smiled at everyone. Teachers were always glad to see kids being such good sports.

Marsha knew she should congratulate Roger, too. It *had* been a great kick. But the longer she watched more and more kids congratulate Roger, the less and less she wanted to go over and tell him.

Marsha walked to the back of the line, knowing she was being a poor sport. What a crummy day it had been. In homeroom she had blamed Roger for something he hadn't done. That made her kind of a liar. Miss Murtland and Mrs. Byrnes had both looked disappointed. Now Miss Poplin thought she was a poor loser and a bad sport. Marsha sighed. Third grade had just started and she was already getting in so much trouble. Why did these things happen to her, anyway? Bad luck followed Scarlett O'Hara around, too. Maybe having a wild temper was some sort of curse. Maybe a witch had cast an evil spell on her when she was a little baby.

Marsha sighed. She knew there weren't any witches in real life. She looked around the gym. There weren't any real witches, but there *was* Roger. He was real. A real pain in the neck. He had probably put some sort of curse on her back in first grade with that dead snake. Yeah, it had to be his fault.

Roger was the only one who enjoyed seeing her this unhappy. Marsha followed the line back to homeroom. She would have to make Roger take back his dead-snake curse before it ruined her whole third-grade year. Maybe her whole life!

Chapter Eight

The next day at lunch, Marsha told Collette and Sarah about the curse.

"A dead-snake curse?" Collette and Sarah started to laugh. "Marsha, you're nuts!"

Marsha frowned at her two friends. Boy, did it make her mad to share a private secret with them and then have them laugh at her. "Think about it, girls," Marsha said slowly. "My rotten, bad luck in school started way back in the first grade. Remember when Sister Lucille yelled at me for eating red crayons? Then in second grade I had to sit in the corner because I accidentally spilled orange juice in the fish tank." Marsha shook her head. "And I was always getting lost in the halls."

Collette smiled. "So? You were just a normal little kid getting used to school. What does a dead snake have to do with it?"

Marsha pounded her fist down on the table. "Because none of the trouble I get into is ever *my* fault. It's all because Roger Friday put that runover snake in my locker. It's jinxed my whole school career. Everyone knows a dead snake is bad luck."

Sarah and Collette started to giggle.

"Oh, stop laughing," Marsha snapped. "If you two were really my good, best friends, you would want to help me."

Collette patted Marsha on the shoulder. She wasn't smiling now. She looked kind of worried, like she finally believed Marsha. "We *are* your good friends. I don't believe in dead-snake curses. But I'll be glad to help."

"Me, too," added Sarah. "But I thought it was a black cat on Halloween that was supposed to be bad luck."

Marsha smiled. "I'm sure Roger knew he

would get in a lot more trouble if he tried to sneak a black cat into school." Marsha was feeling better already. She was lucky to have such good friends. With three of them working against Roger, they would win. "Now you two go up to Roger and ask him to call off the curse. Tell him my uncle knows a policeman and he'll come here in his squad car if — "

Collette laughed, then covered her mouth. "Sorry, Marsha. I feel silly talking about this snake curse. Roger will think we're nuts."

Marsha shook her head, trying hard to keep her temper all wrapped up. Collette was the smartest girl in the third grade, but she didn't know a thing about Roger. "We have to scare Roger."

Sarah grinned. "Are you sure Roger even remembers putting that dead snake in your locker?"

"Of course he does!" snapped Marsha. "How many times does somebody put a runover smelly snake in somebody's locker? Roger did it on purpose so I would get yelled at my whole life. I never did a thing to him."

Sarah rolled her eyes, "Well, you did put soap chips in Roger's peanut butter sandwich last year . . ."

Collette nodded. "And you put an alarm clock inside his desk in the first grade, and — "

Marsha waved her hands up and down. Why did she have to have best friends with perfect memories? Sure there were a *few* times when she tried to get back at Roger for some crummy thing he did to her. She had to stick up for herself, didn't she? Her mother was always telling her not to let a crowd tell her what to do. "Think for yourself!" was what she always said.

"Listen, I was only a little kid then." Marsha sat up straighter. She gave them both a nice smile so they could tell she didn't have any mean tricks in store for Roger. "I promised my parents that I wouldn't get in any more trouble, okay? I even signed this contract. Let's just make Roger behave so I can be good, okay?"

Marsha was glad to see Sarah and Collette nod.

"Now, here comes old Roger now. I'll go throw away my lunch bag. You guys ask him to call off his snake curse. Tell him to eat a frog or swallow worms or whatever he has to do to erase the first curse. . . . Tell him I won't bother him for the rest of my life if he will."

"What if he doesn't know what we're talking about?" asked Collette. "I mean, he put that dead snake in your locker years ago, and — "

Marsha groaned. "Please, just *ask* him, okay? Trust me, every morning when Roger Friday wakes up, he plans how he will get me in trouble. That kid will know exactly what you're talking about."

Marsha hopped out of her seat and grabbed her lunch bag and milk carton. She passed Roger and his two friends on the way to the trash can.

"Oh, leaving so soon, Marsha?" asked Roger. "I hope it was something I said."

Roger's buddies laughed. Roger's face got red, the way it did when he was getting lots of attention.

Marsha's mouth opened. She was about to tell Roger to go jump in the trash can, but she didn't. Right now she didn't want to get him mad. If he got too mad, he might not take back the snake curse.

Instead, Marsha just smiled nicely and walked past. When she saw how shocked Roger looked, she almost laughed.

Marsha took her time dropping her napkin, orange rind, and bread crusts into the trash can, so she could watch Collette and Sarah walk over to Roger. Collette was talking first. That was good. Collette was so smart. She would know just the right words to make Roger call off his snake curse.

Roger's head swung around. He stared at Marsha. Marsha nearly toppled into the trash can, she was so nervous. Then Roger took off his glasses and stared at Marsha some more. Finally he put on his glasses and turned back to talk to Sarah.

"What is taking so long?" wondered Marsha. She let a few potato chips drop into the trash can. In a few seconds, her lunch bag would be empty and she would have to walk back to the table. She didn't want to walk back while they were still talking.

Marsha's heart started to beat faster and faster as Collette and Sarah walked toward her. Collette was frowning. Sarah looked puzzled.

"Oh no," whispered Marsha. Her hands shook. She grabbed onto the trash can. What had Roger said? Maybe he was so mad now he would put *another* snake curse on her. She would have bad luck for the rest of her life!

"What did he say?" Marsha cried.

Collette looked up. She glanced back at Roger who was busy talking and laughing again. "He said he didn't know what we were talking about."

Sarah frowned. "Yeah. Boy, did we sound stupid."

"What? Why?" Marsha's heart was beating even faster.

Collette reached out and patted Marsha on the arm. "Roger didn't put that dead snake in your locker. He said it was Kenny Scholtz."

Sarah closed her eyes. "I felt so stupid."

Marsha felt worse than stupid. If Roger hadn't put some awful curse on her, then why did she get in so much trouble? And if it wasn't Roger's fault, then . . . Marsha swallowed hard. Her whole mouth tasted sour. If it wasn't Roger's fault, then maybe . . . maybe, her wild temper was the curse!

Chapter
<u>Nine</u>

After recess, Miss Murtland stood out in the hall while Room 10 went to the water fountain. She leaned against the wall, laughing and talking with each student. Marsha was a little nervous. What if Miss Murtland didn't want to talk to her? What if she thought Marsha was mean for blaming Roger? Marsha chewed on her thumbnail and watched as Miss Murtland mussed up Roger's hair and laughed. Boy, Miss Murtland seemed to like Roger a lot. More than she liked Marsha. What if Miss Murtland told Marsha to skip her drink and go right inside the class?

"I'm sorry, Marsha, but there isn't enough water for liars!"

Marsha closed her eyes and said a quick prayer. "Please, God. Let Miss Murtland still like me. Let me keep my temper in and grow a good heart . . ."

Marsha's eyes flew open as someone whacked her hard on the back.

"Hey, not falling asleep in line are you, Marsha?"

Marsha spun around. There was Roger Friday, laughing at her.

Roger wiggled his eyebrows up and down. "You already fell asleep in gym class. Thanks to you, we won!"

A few kids laughed. Miss Murtland looked confused, but then smiled as if it had to be a joke. She clapped her hands. "Okay, children, let's hurry up. Reading class is about to begin."

Marsha waited in line, hoping she was still allowed to get a drink. Miss Murtland hurried the other children into the class-room. Lorraine, Matt, and Marsha all got drinks without Miss Murtland standing beside the water fountain, laughing and talking.

Marsha took a small sip. The water would have tasted a lot better if Miss Murtland had still been there. She could have held back Marsha's hair, or asked if she was having a good day.

Marsha choked and wiped some water from her chin. She *wasn't* having a good day. Not one drop of it had been good so far. Marsha stood up and walked into the classroom. Oh well, it was only twelve–fifteen. There was still lots of time left for the day to turn good. Her mother was always telling her that it wasn't what the day gave you, it was what you did with the day.

Marsha smiled at Mrs. Byrnes and Miss Murtland as she walked by.

"Did you both have a good lunch?" Marsha asked.

"Yes, thank you," said Miss Murtland. She put her hand with the jiggly bracelets on Marsha's shoulder. "How about you?"

Marsha nodded. It probably wasn't a good idea to tell her teachers about the dead-snake curse. Besides, even though her fresh start had wilted a little, there was still time to perk it up again.

As soon as everyone was seated, Miss Murtland walked to the front of the class. Her smile looked kind of nervous.

Marsha sat up straighter and smiled back. This was the first class Miss Murtland was teaching all by herself.

Mrs. Byrnes gathered up her black planning book, pencils, and a stack of spelling papers. "Well, I'll leave you all alone now. Have fun."

The room was absolutely quiet as everyone watched Mrs. Byrnes go out the door. Miss Murtland drew in a deep breath and smiled again. Marsha was pretty sure she saw the thin bracelets jingle a little as Miss Murtland's hand shook.

"Now, I thought we could talk about some of the books y'all have read."

Nobody raised their hand. Marsha looked

around, half raising her hand. Did Miss Murtland ask a question, or was she just getting warmed up?

Miss Murtland must have thought she had asked a question because she held up both arms. "Surely y'all have been reading over the summer."

Marsha leaned forward. Was this a question?

Miss Murtland squeezed her hands together and smiled again. "Did *anybody* read a book?"

Everyone's hand shot up. Marsha waved hers back and forth. Boy, Miss Murtland looked so happy now, like she finally found out how to teach.

Miss Murtland sat on the edge of the desk, the way Mrs. Byrnes did. "Michael, tell me about your book."

"I forget the title, but it was so cool. This guy was on a real weak baseball team and he wanted to quit, but his mom said he couldn't, cause then he would be a quitter and grow up to be a bum, and . . ." Michael stopped to swallow. "Then this crummy coach, that nobody wanted, came and coached them and they got good and won the Series."

Miss Murtland grinned. "Sounds good. That sounds like a real nice book, Michael. Can you try to think of the title and tell us tomorrow?"

Michael looked worried. "Is this homework?"

Miss Murtland laughed and then lots of kids laughed, too.

Miss Murtland called on Jennifer next. Marsha leaned forward, waving her arm and groaning. Wait till Miss Murtland heard what she had to say.

" . . . and then the little girl thanked her grandmother and went back to New York to live," finished Jennifer.

"Marsha, what book did you read?" Miss Murtland had her arms crossed and a yellow pencil behind her ear. She was still as pretty as Wendy Dixon, the weather girl, but she looked exactly like a real teacher.

Marsha stood up. "I read a very grown-up book this summer."

Roger turned around and laughed. "So you finally made it through *The Three Little Pigs*, huh?"

Marsha shook back her hair and looked right up at Miss Murtland. She wasn't going to pay a speck of attention to rude Roger. Once Miss Murtland heard about her grown-up book, she would know that Marsha was a very good student. Maybe the best reader in the whole third grade.

Miss Murtland stood up and took a step closer to Marsha. "What is the title, Marsha?"

Marsha felt like laughing out loud, she was so excited. "This summer, my gramma and I read *Gone With the Wind*."

Marsha kept her eyes glued to Miss Murtland's face, waiting to see her huge smile. Miss Murtland looked surprised. "You read *Gone With the Wind*? By Margaret Mitchell?"

Marsha nodded. Maybe Miss Murtland would be so impressed, she would write a special paper on Marsha. "Third-Grader Reads Hardest Book in the World!"

Marsha could tell Miss Murtland was

trying to think of something special to say. Her cheeks were getting pinker and pinker.

"Now, did your grandmother read that book to you, Marsha?" asked Miss Murtland.

Marsha smiled and shook her head. "No, I read it all by myself. I read all about Scarlett O'Hara and how brave she was. I read all about the Civil War and the fighting and — "

Miss Murtland held up her hand. "I saw the movie." Miss Murtland scratched her head and then smiled at Marsha. "I hope you had a chance to read some good *children's* books this summer, too, Marsha. Adult books will be waiting for you in years to come. You really shouldn't be reading such hard books right now."

Marsha's cheeks felt warm, like she was getting a fast fever. Miss Murtland wasn't a bit excited about Marsha reading *Gone With the Wind*. In fact, she was almost acting as if she didn't believe Marsha had read it.

Marsha slid back down in her seat. She *had* read *Gone With the Wind*. At least a page or two. Maybe five. And she had read every word on the videocassette boxes. Marsha sighed and tugged at her hair. Miss Murtland would have been happier if she had told her she had read *Little Teddy Bear Sings a Song*, or *Humpty Dumpty Falls Off a Wall* . . . baby books.

Marsha felt her desk shake. She looked up. There was Roger Friday. Looking right in her face.

"Did you really read that book?" he asked.

Marsha thought about kicking the back of his chair so he would turn around. But then she remembered that was her wild temper talking. So she just nodded at Roger as if he were a normal person.

Roger kept staring at her. "*Wow!* My mom read that book and it took her about a zillion years. It's the thickest book my mom owns."

Marsha just shrugged. She *wanted* to say, "Well, so what? Maybe I'm smarter than your mother."

But Miss Murtland might hear. So Marsha just said, "Oh," and waited for Roger to turn around. Marsha was proud of herself. If she could only remember to swallow mean things, instead of saying them, she would grow a good heart fast. Before Miss Murtland had to leave Room 10.

Chapter
<u>Ten</u>

When reading class was almost over, Miss Murtland handed out candy corn. She gave everyone a little plastic Baggie, filled with corn and tied with a bright orange ribbon.

"Don't wait for Halloween. You can eat the candy now, children," said Miss Murtland. "And while y'all are relaxing, I want you to get together with your buddy."

Marsha stopped chewing. Buddy? Oh no, Miss Murtland wasn't going to have them buddy-up again, was she?

"It will be very interesting to see if you and your buddy can work together on a book report."

"What?" Marsha started choking. She probably just sucked a piece of candy corn into her lungs. How could she work on a book report with Roger? That kid probably only read comic books . . . or pop-up books with lots of pictures and no words.

"Are you all right, Marsha?" Miss Murtland hurried down the aisle. "Do you need a drink?"

Marsha shook her head and wiped her watery eyes. She didn't need a drink of water. She needed a new buddy.

"Work together for the next five minutes, discussing books you have both read. List your favorite books. Have your buddy list his or her favorite books. Then the two of you decide which book you want to do a report on." Miss Murtland smiled. "Are there any questions?"

Marsha bit the white cap off her candy corn. Doing a book report with Roger would be awful.

"Yes, Roger?" said Miss Murtland.

"My buddy is Marsha. I don't have to read *Gone With the Wind*, do I?"

Everyone started laughing. Marsha bit the inside of her lip until her temper stopped flashing red. She raised her hand.

"My buddy is Roger. I don't have to read *Bert and Ernie*, do I?"

Miss Murtland grinned. More children started to laugh. "I am sure you two can agree on at least one book. Now change seats and get to work."

Marsha didn't move a muscle. She watched as Collette and Sarah got up and moved to the back of the room. They sat down on huge pillows and started talking a mile a minute. Matt and J. R. and Elizabeth and Meredith all started working together. Everyone looked so happy. It wasn't fair.

"Well, what books do you like?"

Marsha looked up. Roger was chewing up a whole mouthful of candy corn. His front teeth were orange. He was sitting right on her desk.

"I don't know."

Roger rolled his eyes. "Miss Murtland says we have to think of some books. So think, okay?"

Marsha sighed. "Could you please get off my desk so I can get a piece of paper?"

Roger hopped off. He looked around the room and waved to a couple of kids. They smiled back. Lots of kids liked Roger. Almost the whole class. He liked everyone back. Marsha sighed — everyone but her. What had she ever done to him, anyway?

"So, do you like *Treasure Island*?" Roger asked.

Marsha shook her head. "You never read *Treasure Island*. My cousin just read that and he's in sixth grade."

Roger looked up at the ceiling and smiled. "Oh, yeah. Maybe I just saw the *movie*." He started to laugh.

Marsha poked Roger in the leg with her pencil. "So what's that supposed to mean?"

Roger bent down close. He smelled like candy corn. "It means that you never read *Gone With the Wind*. You just saw the movie."

Marsha leaned back. "I did *too* read it. You can even ask my gramma."

Roger stood up and walked back to his

seat. "Well, I read *Treasure Island*. Let's do our report on that."

Marsha hopped out of her seat. "It would take me a million years to read that book."

Roger's eyebrows started to wiggle. "We have to pick one book. I could never get smart enough to read your book."

Marsha looked up at Miss Murtland. She was busy talking to other groups. She wouldn't like it if she thought Marsha and Roger weren't trying to be good buddies. It would ruin her special paper.

"Well, let's pick another book. A book that we've both already read." Marsha looked at Roger, wondering what he had ever read.

"How about. . . ." Roger stared off into space. "How about *The Kid from Jupiter*?"

Marsha shook her head. "I didn't like that."

"Me, either. That kid was a jerk. He should have stayed on Jupiter."

Marsha grinned. "How about *Wolves That Stalk*?"

Roger twisted in his seat to stare at her.

"That was so dumb. I didn't like the ending."

Marsha's mouth fell open. Collette and Sarah had loved that book. But Marsha hadn't liked the ending, either.

"I really liked this one book. I read it this summer. I read it last year, too."

"What is it?" Marsha hoped Roger wasn't going to name some monster book about chopping people's heads off.

Roger tapped his fingers up and down on his desk. "*Charlotte's Web*. The book was so cool."

Marsha stared at Roger. "You liked *Charlotte's Web*? You liked a story about a pig and a spider being best friends?"

Roger jerked his head up at Marsha and frowned. "Yeah, so what? It was a neat story. Charlotte was smart." He scratched his chin and looked back up at Marsha. "So, what is your favorite book?"

Marsha felt her face flood red. More than anything she wanted to shout *Gone With the Wind*, or *Little House on the Prairie*. But she loved books. She couldn't lie about her favorite, not even to Roger Friday.

"So what is it, Marsha?" said Roger. "You have to tell me sooner or later."

"*Charlotte's Web*," Marsha said quietly.

"No kidding," said Roger. He looked surprised.

"No kidding," said Marsha. She was surprised, too. She never thought she would ever have anything in common with Roger. But they did. They both loved Charlotte.

Chapter
<u>Eleven</u>

"Mom, I still can't believe Roger picked *Charlotte's Web*." Marsha picked up her oatmeal cookie and took a huge bite. "I mean, I thought he was going to pick some stupid book like, *How to Swallow Live Fish*, or *Monster Monday*."

Marsha's mother put some more warm cookies on the table. "Why aren't you happier? Now you get to work on a report about a book you both love."

"I know. But part of me feels funny. Roger has been a pain in the neck for years. Now I find out he likes my favorite book.

What if we both like the same songs? The same television shows?"

Marsha's mother laughed. "So? It just means that maybe you two could be friends. If you stopped fighting long enough."

Marsha choked on her cookie. Her eyes got teary. "No way," she managed to sputter out.

Mrs. Cessano just smiled. She put away the milk. Marsha's mother never made Marsha pretend to be friends with anyone. "You can't be rude or mean to them," her mother always said. "But pretending to like someone a lot, when you don't at all, isn't honest."

Marsha dipped the end of her cookie in her milk. Actually, she wasn't sure if she liked Roger or not. She was sure she didn't like him at all when he was busy getting her in trouble. But other times, Roger could be so funny that Marsha *did* like him. He had a great sense of humor. Marsha thought that people who wrote funny movies must have been Roger-type kids when they were little. Or the ones who invented glow-in-the-dark teeth, or rubber noses that played jingle bells . . . neat people.

"Hey, you didn't fall asleep on me, did you?" Marsha's mother bent down and gave her a kiss. "Why don't you go and play with Collette for a while?"

Marsha nodded, wondering if her daydreaming meant her brain was being overworked. It was hard to keep her wild temper in. Marsha smiled. Wait till her gramma Hughes came down to visit. Marsha would make sure that they sat on the couch together to watch *Gone With the Wind*. Halfway through the movie, Gramma would turn to Marsha and say, "Hey, you aren't like Scarlett O'Hara at all anymore. You're much too sweet, Marsha."

Marsha smiled. Her chest tingled. That must be because she was growing a good heart.

"I think I'll go upstairs and start my book report, Mom."

"What?" Mrs. Cessano looked at the oven clock. "Honey, you just got home from school. Don't you want to play first?"

Marsha picked up her book bag. "No. Miss Murtland was real proud that Roger and I had picked a book so fast. She let us go to the library to take out a copy of *Charlotte's Web*."

"Great."

"But Roger said he already had his own copy at home." Marsha leaned back in her chair. "Roger was real excited when he was talking about his book. He said it was the first hardback book anyone ever bought him. He keeps it up on the shelf over his bed so his little sister can't get her grubby little hands on it."

"I didn't know Roger had a little sister," said Marsha's mother.

"Yeah. She's only five. I don't know her name. Roger said he named his gerbils Wilbur and Charlotte."

Marsha looked up at her mother. "Roger kept talking and talking about the book. He remembered Templeton's name and the sheep's name." Marsha shook her head. She loved the book, too, but she hadn't memorized it like Roger. Marsha felt her heart beat a little faster. What if Roger knew more about the book than she did? What if Miss Murtland gave Roger an A and Marsha only got a C for her half of the report?

What if Miss Murtland ended up liking Roger best?

Chapter
<u>Twelve</u>

Marsha worked extra hard in school for the next week. She was the last one standing in the spelling bee. Her math paper hung up above the chalkboard. And on Wednesday, Miss Murtland loved Marsha's map of Pennsylvania so much, she held it up for the whole class to see. Marsha couldn't stop smiling. Third grade was fun. It was getting easier to stay out of trouble. Not one teacher had yelled at her for days.

"What's so funny?"

Marsha looked up. Roger was standing next to her desk.

"Your face," Marsha said. She slapped

her hand over her mouth and looked around the room. What if Miss Murtland had heard?

"Come on, Marsha. We have to think of a cover for our book report." Roger let his markers roll across Marsha's desk. "And I hope you wrote something about the book. I have three pages written already. I'm doing all the work."

Marsha nodded. Roger was right. His three pages were really good, too. He told why Charlotte was his favorite character. He said he liked Fern, because Fern loved animals as much as he did.

"So do you have any ideas?" Roger asked.

"Sorta." Marsha was going to tell why Wilbur the pig was her favorite character. But every time she sat down to write something about the book, she couldn't. Everything Roger wrote was funny and good. Yesterday Miss Murtland picked up his paper and read it to the whole class. All three pages. She laughed out loud twice. Then she patted Roger on the head and said he was a born writer.

"What's wrong with you?" asked Roger.

He poked her in the shoulder with his finger. "You look like you're going to throw up or something."

Marsha sat up straighter and tried to look very healthy. She didn't want Miss Murtland sending her down to the nurse's office. The school nurse had enough work. She always had piles of papers on her desk and at least two little kids with red faces sitting on stools or lying on the green plastic couch.

"I'm okay," Marsha said. "I was thinking about the book report. It's due tomorrow."

Roger knocked on Marsha's head. "Wake up! I know it's due tomorrow. Why do you think I've been asking you for your half of the report? Let me see what you have so far."

Marsha put her hand over her paper. "No, not yet." Her paper wasn't good. She didn't want Roger or Miss Murtland to read it. Miss Murtland would like Roger's report much better. His half would get an A and Marsha's half would get a big, fat F.

"Oh my," Miss Murtland would say. "This isn't good enough to be in Roger's report. Please do it over again and then go stand in the corner."

Roger tried to pull Marsha's paper away. "Come on, Marsha. You're smart. Your book report will sound smart."

Marsha leaned over her paper. "Don't touch it. I'm not ready yet."

"I just want to see it!" Roger gave one final tug and Marsha heard the rip.

"Sorry," Roger said quickly.

"Oh, good grief — now look what you've done!" cried Marsha. "Thanks a lot, Roger."

Roger held up a tiny bit of paper. "Look, it's only the corner. You can tape that back on."

Marsha looked down at her paper. It only had two sentences on it. Two dumb sentences that weren't good at all.

"Here, I'll tape it," offered Roger.

Before he could touch it again, Marsha grabbed her yellow sheet of paper and wrinkled it. Then she ripped the paper up.

"Hey, what's going on?" asked Miss Murtland. She left Sarah and Collette's team and hurried over.

Before Miss Murtland could reach out for the pieces that used to be a book report, Marsha threw them on the floor.

"Roger ripped my book report," Marsha said in a whisper.

"What?" cried Roger.

"What?" asked Miss Murtland. She sounded angry.

Lots of kids hurried over. They all wanted to see who was going to get in trouble. Marsha looked up and saw Miss Murtland's mad face and Roger's sad face. Things were happening too fast.

"I will not allow students to rip up book reports," announced Miss Murtland. "Part of my job is to teach y'all to be nice people."

Collette and Sarah nodded. Roger shrugged. And Marsha started to cry.

Chapter Thirteen

Miss Murtland asked Collette to please take Marsha down to the girls' room.

"Roger is in so much trouble," cried Marsha. She walked over to the sinks and turned on the cold water. "Miss Murtland said Roger's bad behavior might ruin her buddy system project. Did you see Roger's face when she told him he was going to have to go talk to Sister Mary Elizabeth? I feel sorry for him."

"Don't feel sorry for Roger, Marsha," said Collette. "He deserves to be in trouble. I can't believe he ripped up your whole report." Collette held back Marsha's braids as she splashed more water on her face. "The report is due tomorrow. It was nice of Miss Murtland to say you could hand yours in a day late."

"I know." When Marsha looked up in the mirror, her face was full of bright red patches.

"You really cried hard, Marsha." Collette handed her a paper towel.

"I didn't think I was ever going to stop." Marsha was glad Miss Murtland had allowed Collette to go to the girls' room with her to calm down. A mean teacher might have just sent her down to the nurse's office to rest on the couch.

"Why did Roger do it?" Collette crossed her arms and leaned against the sink. "Gosh, Miss Murtland is so mad."

Marsha didn't answer. She was too busy remembering the big fat lie she had told. Tears flooded her eyes. Why was it so easy to lie, anyway?

"Marsha, what's wrong now? Do you want me to go get the nurse?"

Marsha took a deep breath and shook her

head. She would be all right. She just had to get used to the fact that she had ruined everything. All those days and days of trying to be nice and kind. All those days and days of growing a good heart. It was all gone. Why did lies just pop into her head like that?

Collette put her arm around Marsha. "Please don't cry, Marsha. Miss Murtland said Roger has to stay after school for three days in a row. I heard Miss Murtland say she would have to call his parents."

"They shouldn't do that!" Marsha's heart started to beat faster. Parents always asked lots of questions. Too many questions.

"Because Roger didn't answer any of Miss Murtland's questions," said Collette. "He's probably scared that he was caught doing something bad."

Marsha still couldn't understand why Roger hadn't told Miss Murtland the truth. He just stood there. He looked real sad. But he never said, "Marsha is lying again."

Marsha tossed her paper towel in the trash can. Why did she do such dumb stuff, anyway? Scarlett O'Hara had lied lots in the movie. But she was starving and needed lots of money. Sometimes she needed to marry someone real fast. That's why she lied. Marsha frowned. Even Scarlett was wrong to lie. She made lots of people sad, too.

Marsha turned off the water. Before the lie could get another minute older, she was going to tell Miss Murtland the truth.

"Marsha, do you feel okay now?" Collette hurried to catch up. "Do you want to get a drink of water?"

Marsha shook her head. "No. I have to talk to Miss Murtland right away."

Collette patted Marsha on the shoulder. "Tell her that you worked real hard on the report. Tell her you probably would have gotten an A on it."

Marsha stopped outside the classroom door. She was a little nervous. Maybe she should try her speech out on Collette first. Kind of a dress rehearsal for Miss Murtland.

"Collette, I don't think Roger should be in all this trouble," Marsha began. "I mean, it was only one page."

Collette's eyes grew wide. "Yeah, but that one page was your book report. You always said he bugged you on purpose, Marsha. Now I finally believe you."

"You do?"

Collette nodded. "Yeah. I mean, sometimes Sarah and I thought that you were making things up. About Roger always trying to get you in trouble. But now we know you were telling the truth." Collette patted Marsha's arm. "Sarah and I will always believe you now, Marsha. Honest."

Marsha felt a lump in her throat. Telling lies was hard work. Once you told one, you had to keep telling them so no one found out about the first one. If she told Collette that she had lied about Roger and the ripped report, Collette would never believe her again. Collette might tell Sarah not to believe Marsha ever again, too. What if her two best friends decided to stop being her friends at all? Who wants to be friends with someone who makes up double-decker lies?

Marsha put her hand on the classroom door. The door opened and Miss Murtland

and Roger walked out. Marsha jumped back and hid behind Collette. Roger had probably told Miss Murtland the whole truth while she was in the girls' room with Collette. Maybe he stood up on the teacher's desk and rolled a piece of paper into a loudspeaker. "Attention . . . attention. Listen, everyone. Marsha Cessano is the real liar and paper ripper. Her fingerprints are all over the report. My fingerprints are only on the tiny tip."

Maybe Miss Murtland believed Roger right away. "Oh Roger, forgive me for yelling at you!" Miss Murtland probably hugged Roger. "Poor, poor Roger Friday. Let's go find Marsha and yell at her together."

"Marsha . . . sugar, are you o-kay?" Miss Murtland was shaking Marsha's shoulder.

Marsha blinked. Miss Murtland was bent down, looking into her face. Marsha could smell Miss Murtland's sweet strawberry-smelling shampoo. "I'm okay."

Marsha glanced over at Roger. He looked right back at her. His face wasn't wearing any look. It was like someone had erased everything, except for his sad eyes.

Miss Murtland stood up straighter. "Now y'all go back inside with Mrs. Byrnes. Roger and I are going down to the office so he can call his momma." Miss Murtland put one hand on Roger's shoulder and the other on Marsha's. "I am real unhappy that y'all aren't better buddies."

Roger shoved both hands in his pockets. His chin dropped. The tips of his ears went from pink to red. Marsha opened her mouth. Now was when she should tell everyone what really happened. Before Roger got yelled at by Sister Mary Elizabeth and then his very own mother.

"Miss Murtland . . . I . . ." Marsha took a step forward.

Miss Murtland and Roger both turned. Roger looked up. He took his hands out of his pocket like something was about to happen.

"Yes, Marsha?" Miss Murtland asked.

Collette patted Marsha on the back again. Miss Murtland smiled sweetly. Her silver bracelets jingled as she pushed back her pretty hair. "What, sugar?"

Marsha chewed her bottom lip. Once she told everyone she was the real liar, no one would be smiling at her. No one would call her "sugar." Miss Murtland would probably march her right off to Father Walter's confessional booth.

"Oh. . . . Nothing," said Marsha softly.

Miss Murtland raised an eyebrow. Roger's chin dropped down again. Then they both turned and marched down toward Sister Mary Elizabeth's office.

Chapter Fourteen

Roger and Miss Murtland didn't come back during art. They still weren't back when Mrs. Byrnes announced it was time to line up for lunch. Marsha didn't say a word the whole way down to the cafeteria. Even when she was sitting between Collette and Sarah, she felt lonely. She felt just like Scarlett O'Hara had after she had lied to handsome Rhett Butler for the tenth time.

"Let's hurry and eat so we can go outside. It's really warm today. Let's put our jackets on the hedges and play four square."

"I don't feel like playing." Marsha pushed

her lunch bag away. "And I'm not hungry, either."

"How about an oatmeal cookie?" Sarah offered. "My grandma made them last night."

Marsha tried to smile. "No, thanks. Roger has been in the office for a long time."

Collette scooted closer to Marsha. "I know. Richie said that when he went to get extra scissors from the art closet, he saw Roger sitting on a chair in the office." Collette took a big sip of milk. "And he said that Sister kept pointing to the black phone on the secretary's desk. 'Call your mother,' Sister kept saying."

Marsha grabbed Collette's arm. "Did he call her?"

Collette shook her head. "No. Richie said that Roger just kept saying, 'No.' "

All three girls gasped. Wow! Nobody said no to Sister Mary Elizabeth.

"I bet Roger's dad is going to kill him," Sarah said.

"What?" Marsha was worried. Was Roger's dad mean? She had only seen Roger's mother once or twice at Open House. She was short with curly red hair. She had real white teeth and pale blue glasses. She was always smiling. She couldn't be mean.

"I heard that Roger's dad used to wrestle alligators," added Collette. "Roger said once that his dad was stronger than those wrestlers on TV."

Sarah laughed. "Yeah. But now we know that Roger Friday is a big liar. So maybe his dad is really a little skinny guy. Maybe he can't even open a mayonnaise jar."

Marsha licked her lips and tried to swallow. But what if Roger's dad was someone with a temper? What if he got so mad at Roger for ripping up reports and saying no to a nun that he screamed at Roger for an hour? What if he was so mean that he threw Roger's stuff out in the trash?

"Poor Roger," whispered Marsha.

Collette nodded. "Yeah. I bet he isn't allowed to go on the field trip with us next week. Roger won't get to see how they make ketchup or pickles at the Heinz factory."

Sarah shook her head. "He'll be too busy helping Mr. Doyle clean gum off the bleachers."

Marsha picked up her lunch bag and stood up.

"Where are you going?" asked Collette.

Marsha shrugged. She wasn't sure. But she was getting real worried. Worried about Roger. He was still a pain in the neck. He made it impossible for Marsha to grow a good heart. But he was in lots and lots of trouble now.

"I'm going to ask Miss Murtland something." Marsha raced out of the cafeteria. She pounded up the worn marble stairs, her lunch bag banging against her hip. Maybe she could tell Miss Murtland that she didn't want to "press charges" against Roger. People did it all the time on TV. Then Sister Mary Elizabeth would let Roger go back to class.

At the top of the stairs, Marsha turned left. The door to the principal's office was closed. Marsha could hear lots of talking. Some of it was yelling.

Marsha ducked behind the huge statues of Mary and St. Joseph. The door of the principal's office opened. Lots of people came out in a long single line. First came Miss Murtland. She was shaking her head. Next came Roger's mother. She still had the red curly hair and the blue glasses. But her smile was gone. Next came Roger. He looked mad. He had his coat on and a stack of books. Sister Mary Elizabeth was at the end of the line.

" . . . and when you are ready to talk about what happened, Roger, then you will come back into the third grade."

Marsha felt cold prickles running down her back. Roger was being kicked out of the third grade!

"I'm sure he will feel like talking soon," Roger's mother replied. She looked at Roger and put her arm around his shoulder. "This isn't like my Roger."

Marsha watched as Mrs. Friday and Roger walked slowly down the wide steps and out the door. Marsha hid behind the statues even more. She didn't want Miss

Murtland or Sister to see her now. She listened to the glass doors bang closed and heard the *click-click*ing of Miss Murtland's heels as she walked back down the hall. Sister Mary Elizabeth closed her heavy office door. The hall was quiet. Everything seemed too quiet now that Roger was gone. Marsha closed her eyes. She was feeling mixed up inside. For years, she had hoped that Roger would be kicked out of school. For years, that had been her favorite wish.

So why doesn't it feel good? thought Marsha. Why do I feel so bad?

Chapter
<u>Fifteen</u>

After lunch, Miss Murtland passed out papers about the field trip. "We will leave on Tuesday at nine o'clock and be back by one." She wrote *Heinz* on the blackboard. "I'm sure we will have lots of fun."

Sarah waved her hand. "Can we sit wherever we want on the bus?"

"Sure," said Miss Murtland. "But be sure and stay with your buddy."

Some kids groaned. Most kids cheered. Marsha leaned forward and stared at Roger's empty desk. He wouldn't be back in school for the field trip. Marsha would have to sit all by herself.

"Can Marsha sit with Sarah and me?" asked Collette.

"Or she can sit with Megan and me!" offered Lorraine.

Miss Murtland glanced at Roger's empty desk, too. "Well, let me think about that for a while, girls. But aren't y'all sweet to concern yourselves?"

Marsha smiled at Collette and Lorraine. She felt kind of funny. Everyone was being so nice to her. But they were only being nice because they thought Roger had been mean. Marsha knew that she hadn't really earned their niceness. But she didn't know how to give it back.

When the bell rang to line up for buses, Marsha was the first one out of her seat. She couldn't wait for the day to end. Maybe once she got home, she could think of a plan to get herself out of this mess. She didn't want Roger to be in trouble. But she didn't want to be in trouble, either.

Maybe she could call up Roger's mother and pretend to be Sister Mary Elizabeth.

"Please forgive us for yelling at your nice son," Marsha could say in a deep voice. "We found out that he did not rip up that sweet Marsha Cessano's paper after all. A robber ripped it up. But the police have arrested him so Roger can come back to school."

Marsha nodded. That sounded great. Then she frowned. But what would the real Sister Mary Elizabeth say when Roger walked into school? Marsha pulled on her braid, thinking. Maybe she would have to call Sister Mary Elizabeth and pretend to be Roger's mother. "Sister, my son has promised never, ever to rip up Marsha's papers again. Please let him back in school."

"Bus seventeen, bus twenty-six . . ." called out Miss Merkle over the intercom.

Marsha walked slowly down the hall, her book bag almost dragging on the floor. She couldn't use any of those plans. Each one was a lie.

"No more lying," Marsha promised herself. Lies only made it worse.

I have to think of another plan, thought Marsha. That might be hard. Because this plan would have to be special. A plan that would get Roger out of trouble and not get Marsha into trouble. Marsha hurried to the bus, hoping she could think up a plan on the way home. Before it was too late.

Chapter Sixteen

When the bus pulled to a stop, Marsha got off. She waved good-bye to Collette and walked slowly up the street. She still didn't know what she was going to do about Roger.

Marsha walked up her front steps. She twisted the large brass door knob. It was locked. A tiny yellow square of paper was taped to the milkbox.

DEAR MARSHA,

HI SWEETIE!! I HAD TO RUN INTO TOWN TO GIVE DADDY

HIS BRIEFCASE. GO OVER TO
THE MURPHYS' AND PLAY WITH
COLLETTE UNTIL I GET BACK. I
SHOULD BE HOME IN AN
HOUR.

LOVE,
MOM

Marsha plunked down on the milkbox.
Oh, no. Now what was she supposed to do?
She wanted to go up in her room and think
up a new plan. Then she wanted to go over
to Roger's and talk to him. Before things
got worse! Marsha looked across the street
at Collette's house. She knew her mother
wanted her to stay over there until she got
back. Playing kickball with Collette would
be more fun than talking to Roger. But it
wouldn't clear up the trouble at school.

Marsha sighed. Why did she keep thinking about Roger, anyway? Marsha chewed
on the end of her braid. Maybe it was because Roger Friday was her only enemy in
life. The only person who really and truly

did not like her. Marsha frowned. Yeah, that had to be it. Well, she didn't like Roger, either.

Marsha hugged her knees. She felt very sad. Not liking someone wasn't very nice. Her parents said all God's children should like each other. Marsha wondered what God really thought of Roger.

Why did Roger always play mean tricks? Like in second grade when he put Jell-O in her coat pockets. Or in first grade when Roger told the whole class that Marsha's grandmother was a witch. He told everyone she rode on a broom. Marsha frowned. Her grandmother didn't ride a broom. She drove a green Volvo with real leather seats. That Roger! He would never change. Marsha would have to keep him as an enemy for the rest of her life. Even when they both grew up and got married to other people. It would still be dangerous to live in the same town as Roger.

"He might poison my kids' dog," said Marsha out loud.

That scared Marsha. It scared her so

much, a plan hopped right into her head. She would make Roger promise not to ever, ever speak to her again. Marsha bent down in her book bag and grabbed a sheet of yellow paper and a pencil. She better write it all out and make Roger sign it.

Marsha raced down her front steps and started to walk quickly down the street, away from her house and away from Browning Road. She wasn't about to let Roger Friday poison her kids' dog in twenty years. She was going to march right over to his house and make him swear, promise with his right hand up to God, that he would never, ever speak to her again. Who knew what Roger would do as he got older and older? One day he would be six feet tall and not afraid of any nuns at Sacred Heart. And then he would remember all the things he wanted to do to Marsha Cessano and come looking for her. He would have a list a mile long, starting with cut off Marsha's braids.

"I've got to talk to Roger right now!" Marsha started running. She was out of breath by the time she reached the stop sign.

She glanced back at her house. Her mom thought she was going to play with Collette until she got back. Marsha drew in a deep breath, wondering if not going to Collette's house was lying. It sounded like it might be. But I have to get Roger out of my life, thought Marsha. Before we both get in more and more trouble.

If she hurried, she would be back before her mother even knew she was gone. Roger only lived three blocks away. On Portland Street.

Marsha started to walk down Highland. She hoped Roger would agree to sign the paper, promising not to talk to her. Maybe he would say no. "You got me in trouble!" Roger might yell. "Get out of my yard."

Marsha stopped. Roger probably *was* mad. He couldn't even go on the field trip. He couldn't even come back to school until he told Sister Mary Elizabeth why he had ripped up Marsha's book report. Marsha twisted her braid around and around until it pinched her head. "First, I'll tell Roger

I'm sorry for lying. Then I'll tell him not to speak to me again."

Up ahead, Marsha could see Mrs. Dock, the crossing guard. She was holding up her large wooden stop sign and waving the children across with her white gloved hand. Marsha started to run faster. Mrs. Dock stayed on the corner of Highland and Hampton until four-fifteen when the middle-school kids got off their bus. That would just be long enough for Mrs. Dock to cross Marsha twice. The first time she crossed her, Marsha would race down Hampton to Portland and talk to Roger. And the second time Mrs. Dock crossed her, Marsha would be so happy, she would fly across Highland Avenue. It would all be over; Roger Friday would be out of Marsha's life forever. Marsha grinned and started to run down the street. Her tennis shoes crunched on the leaves and her braids slapped against her back, hurrying her faster and faster. Only two more blocks to Portland Street. Marsha didn't know Roger's house number. His house would be easy to find. All she had to do was to ask where the troublemaker on the street lived. "Oh, you must mean that ratty Roger Friday," the stranger would say. "Be careful, he's dangerous."

Marsha started to run. Only a few more blocks till the Roger Friday War was over.

Chapter Seventeen

"Thirteen seventeen," said the elderly lady. She leaned across her silver metal fence and pointed with her gardening glove. "Little Rogie Friday lives right there. In the red brick house with the green shutters."

Little Rogie? Marsha laughed. Rogie Friday? "Thank you," giggled Marsha. The old lady pruning her roses didn't frown or laugh when Marsha asked where Roger Friday lived. In fact, the old lady had smiled. Like Marsha had asked where someone normal and nice lived.

She's just old, thought Marsha as she crossed the narrow street. She has forgotten all the times Roger snapped the heads off her flowers. She can't remember him ringing her doorbell ten times and then hiding in the bushes.

Thirteen seventeen was pretty. Marsha shoved her hands in her jumper and stared up at the three-story house. The green shutters weren't hanging off and Roger's silly face wasn't smashed up against the bedroom window. It looked very normal. Marsha glanced down the street. Maybe the old lady was wrong. Surely there had to be a house with spooky green ivy growing over the front door and lots of windows broken by Roger.

"It's not my turn!" came a voice from thirteen seventeen. It was Roger!

"Do it anyway," his mother called. "You're in enough trouble as it is, young man."

"It's not fair!"

Marsha moved behind a huge ivy bush.

Roger's voice sounded like it was ready to crack. Or cry.

The front door opened and Roger came

out, pulling a large reddish dog. Marsha leaned closer. What a strange-looking dog. He looked like a mixture of twenty dogs. His coat was thick and his head was huge. But his legs were really short and skinny. It was the kind of dog a little kid in kindergarten would draw with a fat black crayon.

"It's a good thing you have me, Leaks," grumbled Roger. He led the dog slowly down the sidewalk. "If you waited for Becky to walk you, you'd blow up."

Marsha covered her mouth and giggled. The large dog took tiny steps as if he were wearing high heels. When it reached the hedge, the dog lifted his leg.

"Good boy, Leaks," said Roger. He patted the dog's head. Leaks fell over on his side.

Marsha laughed out loud. Roger's dog was so silly! He couldn't even wet on a bush without falling over.

"Hey!" Roger lifted his dog back on its feet and tugged him toward Marsha. "What are *you* doing here?"

Marsha felt her cheeks flaming. She stepped out from behind the bush. "You don't own the street, do you?"

Roger shook his head. "Nah, but trash pick-up is today, so watch out."

Marsha's mouth fell open. "Yeah, you watch out, too, Roger. That dog looks like it's falling apart."

Marsha stood up straighter. She stepped from foot to foot, like a fighter in the ring. She was ready for Roger. If he threw an insult her way, she would bounce one right back to him.

But Roger just knelt down on one knee and put his arm around Leaks. He leaned his head against the large red head of the dog.

"He doesn't even look like a real dog," added Marsha.

Roger patted Leaks's side. "I know. That's probably why he was ditched."

Marsha felt chills racing up her arms. Right away she knew she had said something dumb, something pure mean. . . .

"I found him in the alley behind Marcus

Drugstore," said Roger. "Last year. Right before Christmas."

"When it snowed so much?" Marsha sat down on the walk next to Roger. Leaks smelled funny, like an old mattress from camp.

"Yeah. Leaks has really skinny legs. They aren't strong enough for him, I guess," said Roger. "So he has a hard time walking around."

"Does he fall over a lot?" asked Marsha. She watched as the big red dog walked around in a slow circle, his tiny paws moving in quick baby steps. Poor dog. He probably couldn't fetch a stick or race up to the bus stop to meet Roger. Marsha felt bad. She shouldn't have laughed at Leaks. He couldn't help looking the way he did.

"He's a nice dog," said Marsha quietly.

Roger smiled and nodded. "He is. If anyone mean gets near me or my sister, Leaks barks his head off."

Marsha leaned back. Could Leaks *smell* meanness? Could he smell the fact that Marsha was mean?

"Once, this big kid from middle school chased me home," said Roger. "Leaks was on the porch, and he took all three steps in one hop, barking and growling."

"Did Leaks fall over?"

Roger nodded. "Yeah, sure. But he got right back up and chased this kid down the block. Leaks is a great dog, all right." Roger slung his arm around Leaks. "He wouldn't bite anyone. But he guards us real good."

Marsha nodded. Leaks was all bark and no bite. Like Roger. Maybe Roger didn't know what a pain in the neck he was.

"So what are you doing down here?" asked Roger. He pulled off a handful of leaves from the hedge and threw them at Marsha's shoes. "You lost?"

"No." Marsha brushed off the leaves. "I came to ask you to sign something."

Roger's face flushed red as if Marsha had just invited him to dance. "Me?"

Marsha nodded. "Yeah. I . . ." Marsha reached out and patted Leaks. He didn't smell so funny now. His fur was thick and furry like a fake bear rug.

"Why do you want to talk to me?" asked Roger. "Probably about the book report. Why did you rip it up, anyway?"

Marsha shrugged, not sure of how she should start this. "I want to . . ." Marsha stopped. She didn't know if she could go on. She hadn't counted on Roger being so nice to his dog, or Roger just sitting on the grass talking like a regular kid. Aside from throwing leaves at her shoes, so far, Roger had been nice. "I don't know. . . . I guess because it was dumb." Marsha frowned. "But I didn't mean for you to get in so much trouble."

Roger just shrugged. "I've been in trouble lots of times. I would have told Miss Murtland you were the one who ripped up the paper, but I did rip it first. Then you just went crazy and kept on ripping."

Marsha nodded. "I guess we both ripped it up."

Roger scratched his head. He shoved his glasses up with his thumb. "Yeah. My mom wants me to tell Sister Mary Elizabeth I ripped it up. I guess I better."

Marsha's eyes grew wide. "Did you tell your mom that I ripped it up, too?"

"I just said I only ripped it once and then it got all wrinkled up." Roger patted Leaks's side like he was a red horse. "I told her I couldn't remember."

"I wrinkled it up," said Marsha quickly.

"Things happened so fast," said Roger. "I wasn't sure so I thought I better keep my mouth shut."

Marsha shivered. Roger had been so brave. He had been scared, too, but he had done the right thing. Marsha felt a pinch of jealousy. Roger had a good heart. And he didn't even know it.

Marsha's hand closed around the yellow paper in her pocket. How was she going to ask Roger to sign her paper now? It would have been better if Roger had been rude to her. It would have been easier if he had squirted Marsha with the hose. "Get off my street, ape face!" That would have made Marsha so mad, she would have been able to shout, "Oh yeah, well promise me you'll never talk to me again, Rogie Pogie!"

But sitting next to Roger and his nice dog was making it a lot harder. Because if Roger promised never to talk to her again, how would Marsha ever find out more about Leaks? And if Roger never talked to her again, how could Marsha ever ask why Roger's little sister never had to walk the dog?

"What did you want me to sign? Something about the book report." Roger scratched a huge bug bite on his leg. His knees were dirty and had lots of scratches on them.

"Yeah, sort of." Marsha knew she would have to hurry up before Mrs. Dock went off duty. Marsha wasn't allowed to cross Highland by herself.

"So what is it?" Roger and Leaks stood up. All three of them walked slowly down the sidewalk.

"I . . . I don't think we should fight in school," said Marsha quickly. "I'm trying to be good."

Roger laughed. "Lots of luck!" Then he stopped smiling. "My mom said if I apologize to Sister and don't get in any more trouble, I can still get a bike for Christmas."

"You don't have a bike?" Marsha stopped. "Everyone has a bike."

Roger shrugged. "Well, the one I have is real old. We had to spend a lot of money trying to fix up Leaks."

Marsha looked down at the fat dog. His tongue was hanging out. He was puffing.

"Leaks has to eat special food and go to

the vet a lot," explained Roger. "My mom says we have the only six-hundred-dollar mutt in town."

Leaks moaned. He toddled over to a scraggly pine tree and lifted his leg. Roger looked up at the sky and waited patiently. Marsha smiled. Roger was nice to give Leaks some privacy. Marsha looked up at the sky, too.

Roger looked back at his house. "I have to get back inside. My mom wants me to call Sister before she leaves school."

"What are you going to tell her about me?" Marsha's heart started to pound.

"Nothing. My mom just said I had to say I was sorry *I* ripped up your report."

"But I ripped up the most," said Marsha. "Are you going to tell her that?"

Roger shook his head. "No. Besides, I did the first rip. I think that was the worst."

Marsha drew in a deep breath. Roger's rip could have been taped back. They both knew that.

"Did you want me to sign something, or not?" asked Roger.

Marsha heard laughter. She turned and saw the flashing lights of the school bus. She was going to have to hurry so Mrs. Dock could cross her back over.

"Oh, that." Marsha tossed back both braids. "I just had a new idea for a cover for our book report, that's all."

Roger smiled. "Good. Show me tomorrow."

"Okay." Marsha leaned down and hugged Leaks. The dog staggered. But he didn't fall.

"See you," said Roger. He gave a gentle tug on the leash and headed toward his house.

"See you," called out Marsha. She started to run, ducking under the low branches and sidestepping a gang of little kids racing down the sidewalk on their hot wheels. A few houses up, Marsha swung her head back, cupping both hands as she hollered to Roger and his dog. "Talk to you, tomorrow. . . . Rogie!"

Marsha could hear Roger laughing. Marsha laughed, too. Then she stopped. Why was she laughing? Once Roger told his side of the story, she would have to tell hers. It was only fair. Tomorrow Roger would be back in the third grade. Would she be out?

Chapter Eighteen

The next morning, Marsha was the first one at the bus stop. She wasn't in a hurry to tell Miss Murtland she had lied, she just wanted to tell Collette first. If Collette still liked her after she knew the truth, maybe Miss Murtland would, too.

As soon as Collette walked up, Marsha grabbed her. She pulled Collette by the arm.

"Collette, I have to tell you something."

Collette smiled. "Is it good news? Is your mom going to have a baby?"

Marsha shook her head. She wished she had some good news to dish out. "No. This is kind of . . . well, *bad* news."

Collette looked sad right away.

"Not real bad," said Marsha quickly. She didn't want Collette to think someone needed an operation. "But remember how Roger ripped up my book report?"

"Yes. I told my mom and she thought it was awful."

Marsha bit her lip. She wished everyone would stop telling their mothers. Mothers got awfully upset about kids breaking the rules.

"Well . . . Roger didn't really rip it up," said Marsha. She stared at her loafers. She was too embarrassed to look at Collette. "I ripped it up, too."

"What?" Collette grabbed onto Marsha's sleeve. "You ripped up your own book report?"

Marsha nodded and nodded. As she nodded, tears began to fall.

"Why?"

Marsha shrugged. Because her report was dumb. Because Miss Murtland liked Roger better. Because Roger made her so mad she couldn't think straight. That's why. Marsha wondered which answer she should give Collette.

"Roger just made me mad. But now I have to tell Miss Murtland the truth," whispered Marsha. "As soon as we get to school. I'll have to tell Mrs. Byrnes the whole story, too."

Collette patted Marsha's arm. "She'll understand. Roger just teased you too much. My brothers drive me nuts, too, Marsha. Just hope Miss Murtland has brothers."

Marsha looked up. Collette didn't sound the least big angry. She sounded like she knew exactly how Marsha felt. Marsha broke into a huge smile. She loved it when people knew how she felt. It made her feelings make sense.

The bus ride to Sacred Heart seemed short. Maybe it was because Marsha kept rehearsing what she was going to say to Miss Murtland. Collette was so nice. She pretended she was Miss Murtland. Every time Marsha told her side of the story, Collette made Miss Murtland smile and say,

"Oh, that's okay, Marsha. I have six brothers so I don't blame you a bit."

But once the school bus pulled up in front of the school, Marsha started to get nervous again. What if Miss Murtland *didn't* have six brothers? What if she fell back in her chair and shouted for Sister Mary Elizabeth?

"Good luck," Collette called as soon as the bus stopped.

Marsha hugged her book bag and walked up the front steps of the school. She hoped Miss Murtland would be alone in the classroom. She wanted to tell her before she told Mrs. Byrnes.

Marsha's heart was pounding so hard, she could feel it drumming against her book bag. What if Miss Murtland sent her to Sister Mary Elizabeth's office? Marsha's heart skipped a beat. What if Miss Murtland frowned and said, "I don't think I like you anymore, Marsha."

When Marsha peeked inside Room 10, she saw that Miss Murtland was alone. She was standing on a chair in front of the bulletin board, stapling pumpkins in a pumpkin patch.

"Hello, Miss Murtland," Marsha said softly. She didn't want to scare her teacher and make her staple her hand.

Miss Murtland turned around. She smiled. "Hi, there, Marsha. How are you doing today?"

"Fine," said Marsha. She wasn't doing fine at all. Miss Murtland looked even younger without her shoes on, just standing on the chair, happy as could be. Marsha didn't want to ruin Miss Murtland's morning. But any minute the kids would come rushing in. Marsha had to tell Miss Murtland the truth *now*.

"Miss Murtland, can I talk to you?" Marsha made her voice grow louder. "It's real important."

Miss Murtland put her stapler down right away. She hopped off the chair, put on her shoes, and walked over to Marsha. Boy, was Miss Murtland a good teacher. She was always ready to listen to a kid.

Marsha's knees almost buckled, as if they

were broken. She wished she felt braver.

"What is it, sugar?" Miss Murtland was so close, Marsha could smell her perfume. Miss Murtland smelled like the bushes in her gramma's yard. The bushes with the purple flowers.

Marsha blinked twice, thinking of how scared Scarlett must have been in the movie, *Gone With the Wind*. In lots of parts of the movie, Scarlett's knees were weak, too. But she made them work.

"Miss Scarlett . . ." Marsha gasped. "I mean, Miss Murtland . . . *I* ripped up my book report."

Miss Murtland's eyebrows went up. "What?"

"Roger ripped up *a little* of my report, but then I ripped up the rest." Marsha swallowed hard. "It was a dumb report. I wanted to rip it. Before you could see how awful it was."

Miss Murtland's eyebrows were still up. Marsha tugged at her braids. She chewed on her lip, and finally started to cry.

"I'm sorry. I should be in the most trouble, not Roger."

Marsha covered her face with her hands. Any minute now, Miss Murtland would start to scream.

"Marsha."

That was all Miss Murtland said. Marsha uncovered one eye. Then the other.

When Marsha finally looked up, Miss Murtland smiled. It wasn't a big smile, but it was big enough to show she wasn't mad at Marsha. It was big enough to show that Miss Murtland still liked her.

"Don't cry." Miss Murtland put her arm around her. Her jangly bracelets played a nice, soft tune.

"I'm sorry," Marsha whispered. "Roger just gets me so mad, sometimes I explode."

Miss Murtland patted Marsha's head. "Well, that can happen. But you have to try harder. Don't let your temper get you in trouble, that's all."

Marsha gulped and nodded. She was already so tired. Telling Miss Murtland the truth took as much energy as playing two games of kickball.

"Thank you for telling me," said Miss Murtland. "That was brave."

"You're welcome," said Marsha. She wanted to say more, but not now. She leaned against Miss Murtland and sighed.

The first morning bell rang. Marsha knew she would have to tell Mrs. Byrnes the truth. Sister Mary Elizabeth, too. Everyone that thought Roger had been to blame.

"I hope you and Roger will still learn how to be good buddies," said Miss Murtland. She gave Marsha a tight hug.

"I'll try," said Marsha.

Marsha thought of the book *Charlotte's Web*. If a spider and a pig could become friends, maybe Roger and Marsha could. In the book, Charlotte spun special messages in her web. She spun *Some Pig*. Marsha thought for a minute. She could make a new book report cover. Maybe she could use lots of black glitter to make a huge spiderweb. And right in the middle, she could print, *Some Buddies!* in gold glitter. It would look great. Roger could do most of the writing, and she could do all the fancy art work.

The morning bell rang. Miss Murtland took off her shoes, got back up on her chair, and started stapling pumpkins. Marsha went over to her desk and got out a fresh sheet of paper. She got out her markers.

By the time the first students came into the classroom, Marsha was halfway finished with her spiderweb. By the time Roger walked in, she was almost done.

Hanging from a tiny thread in the web was a fat little spider wearing a Pirate's baseball cap. The spider had glasses and spiky hair. Next to that thread, hung another spider, a beautiful spider with two long dark braids. The pretty little spider was waving hello with three of her tiny legs.

Marsha stared at the tiny spider with the braids. She was kind of small. You couldn't tell if she was smiling or not.

"Hey, *nice* cover," said Roger. He leaned over next to Marsha.

Marsha bent down closer. Roger liked the

book cover. Marsha was glad. At last she was doing her share of the book report.

The little spiders were nice. Marsha put her finger on top of the pretty spider and smiled. The little girl spider hanging from the web looked great.

Best of all, she looked like she had a very good heart.

About the Author

Colleen O'Shaughnessy McKenna began writing as a child, when she sent off a script for the *Bonanza* series. McKenna is best known for her popular Murphy books, the inspiration for which comes from her own family.

This is Ms. McKenna's eleventh book for Scholastic Hardcover. Her previous titles include: *Too Many Murphys*; *Fourth Grade Is a Jinx*; *Fifth Grade: Here Comes Trouble*; *Eenie, Meanie, Murphy, No!*; *Murphy's Island*; *The Truth About Sixth Grade*; *Mother Murphy*; and *Camp Murphy*.

In addition to the Murphy series, Ms. McKenna has written *Merry Christmas, Miss McConnell!* and the young adult novel, *The Brightest Light*.

A former elementary school teacher, Ms. McKenna lives in Pittsburgh, Pennsylvania, with her husband and four children.